PRELUDE TO MURDER

By
STERLING NOEL

I0541417

ARMCHAIR FICTION
PO Box 4369, Medford, Oregon 97504

REPORT ON MARJORIE LOCHMAN:

"Stewardess by occupation…she continued having a lover after she married…her late husband beat her so severely she often had to be carried to the hospital…his death releases her from bondage to a sadist…"
Could sweet-faced, two-timing Marjorie destroy 48 people to satisfy a black hatred?

SHE HAD THE MOTIVE—
SHE HAD THE MEANS!

This is an unforgettable novel of life and lust and death…of passionate love and even more passionate hate. With a list of suspects a mile long, there is one reporter determined to put all the pieces together, and meeting a deadline is the least of his problems.

POLICE LINE-UP:

PETE MOREHOUSE
He'd been regulated to the basement files, the "morgue" in newspaper patter, but his nose for news was better than ever.

FRAN ADDAMS
An up-n-comer, she was a real go-getter as a far as newswomen went. So why write such a soft sell for such a big story?

LUKE WARDELL
A criminal attorney…for real! His world was turning upside down and his allies were now his enemies.

JUDITH STARR HINEMANN
Possessed of extraordinary beauty and a strong demeanor, men fell for her constantly, at times—literally.

MARJORIE LOCHMAN
Her life was not one of comfort and joy, but had she truly acquired the callousness of a cold-blooded killer?

GORDON BUELL
Looks can be deceiving some say. Was this cool-as-a-cucumber Commish still the legendary fighter he used to be?

VINCENT DICASTRO
He was a dead financier's private secretary—with a key to the grieving widow's rooms!

CHAPTER ONE

FLIGHT 900 OF OCEANIC AIRWAYS vanished in mid-Atlantic on Thursday night, December 5, 1957.

There were forty-eight persons aboard the Triton turbo-prop airliner, one of the newest and most luxurious of the Oceanic Airways fleet. Thirty-seven of these were passengers, nine were crew and two were employees of Oceanic, deadheading to Europe for assignments there.

The last report received from Flight 900 came from a position called 40 West, midway between Gander, Newfoundland, and Shannon, Ireland. At this point the flight was proceeding normally in every way; the plane was functioning perfectly, the weather was ideal for the crossing, with a forty-knot tailwind out of the northwest and radio reception was excellent. The pilot, Captain Fred Lochman, reported these facts in the cryptic code of airways operations, giving in addition the temperature, cloud formations and their altitudes and various gauge readings from his four engines. It was the usual sort of report from 40 West by an airlines captain, meeting all requirements and containing nothing superfluous.

It was the final word received from Flight 900. It was the report made by Captain Fred Lochman. It was the last ever heard from this airliner and the forty-eight souls aboard her.

The bulletin came to the *New York Press* editorial office at 4:30 A.M. over the Associated Press teletype. It read:

AN OCEANIC AIRWAYS LUXURY AIRLINER, FLIGHT 900 FROM IDLEWILD TO PARIS, WAS REPORTED MISSING EARLY TODAY BY OCEANIC AIRWAYS. THE HUGE TRITON TURBO-PROP

PLANE HAD FORTY-EIGHT PASSENGERS AND CREW ABOARD, INCLUDING GRETA FORTUNE, MOTION PICTURE ACTRESS, AND HER HUSBAND, WRITER-PRODUCER MARK CASSELL.   IT LEFT IDLEWILD INTERNATIONAL AIRPORT AT 8:00 P. M. YESTERDAY AND WAS DUE AT ORLY AIRPORT AT NOON (6:00 A.M. NEW YORK TIME) TODAY. LAST REPORT RECEIVED FROM THE AIRLINER WAS FROM A POINT MIDWAY BETWEEN GANDER, NEWFOUNDLAND, AND SHANNON AIRPORT, IRELAND, AND AT THAT TIME (11:35 P.M. NEW YORK TIME) THE FLIGHT WAS PROCEEDING NORMALLY IN EVERY RESPECT, ACCORDING TO OFFICIALS OF OCEANIC AIRWAYS.

OTHER PASSENGERS REPORTED TO BE ABOARD THE MISSING PLANE ARE DR. HARVEY FINSTONE, DIRECTOR OF INTERNATIONAL CHARITIES, AND MRS. FINSTONE, AND LAMAR HINEMANN, FINANCIER WHO LAST WEEK WAS NAMED CHAIRMAN OF THE BOARD OF UNITED POWER.

(EDITOR'S NOTE: A COMPLETE PASSENGER LIST WILL NOT BE AVAILABLE UNTIL 5:00 A.M. AND WILL BE PUT ON THIS WIRE IMMEDIATELY.)

The bulletin was torn off the machine by Carl Yerbe, *Press* office boy, who attended the A.P. and U.P. machines until the regular attendants paid by the press associations came on duty at 6:00 A.M. He started to read it over, lighting a cigarette, and he felt a sudden surge of excitement. This was big. My God, what a story...*Greta Fortune!* He shook out the lighted match in his hand, hardly aware that it had burned his finger, and rushed out of the wire room and across the editorial room to the city desk. He laid the bulletin before Lew Hanford, night city editor, who was correcting a piece of copy from a rewrite man, a cardboard container of black coffee in his left hand.

"Airliner lost," said Yerbe, his excitement sending his voice up to an unnaturally high pitch. "Just came in. Boy, what a story!"

Hanford frowned. He found Carl Yerbe to be an almost constant irritation. He was too eager; he talked too much and too loud; he was always interrupting. If it hadn't been for the Guild, Hanford would have fired him months ago.

"Get me some hot coffee," he said, pushing the container to the edge of the desk.

Yerbe pointed a finger at the dispatch. "Look, aren't you going to—"

"Coffee!" shouted Hanford. "Do you hear me? Coffee! That's all you've got to do right now. Get going."

Yerbe picked up the half-full container and backed away from the city desk. He gave Hanford a brief, malevolent look, then turned and hurried to the elevator that would take him to the lunchroom on the top floor.

Hanford picked up the A.P. bulletin and read it over at a glance. He raised his eyes to the clock facing him above the door to the managing editor's office. Four-thirty-three. The first edition had closed eight minutes ago. He looked around the editorial room, gloomy and nearly deserted at this time of the morning. The two rewrite men, Hal Foster and George Lewbell, were standing, talking, by a window overlooking Park Place. Directly in front of Hanford at the telegraph desk, Pinky Vincent, telegraph editor, was snoring gently, his head in his arms. Pinky could sleep anywhere at any time and often did. To his right, the five copyreaders around the copy desks were reading or talking, all of them with coffee in front of them. Frank Goodman, in the slot, was the only one of these working, going through a batch of copy for the second edition, which would not go to press until 8:00 A.M. Beyond the copy desk the night editor, Sam Crowell, was discussing a picture layout with Phil Rausch, picture editor, and Joe Silvers, head of the art department.

Hanford licked his dry lips, wishing he had a drink. Nine days since he'd gone on the wagon, and this was the worst of all. This was when he really needed it—Ellie in the hospital without a chance in hell to come back to him and the two kids acting like maniacs, refusing to go to Ellie's sister in the Rockaways.

"Sam. We got an airliner lost," he called across to the night editor.

Crowell looked up from the ten-by-twelve photograph of the automobile accident he had been examining. "Yeah? Where?"

"Paris plane. Out over the Atlantic," Hanford replied. "Forty-eight on board. Good names. Greta Fortune was on board."

"Christ," exclaimed Sam Crowell. He looked at his wristwatch and picked up the phone on his desk. "Get me circulation," he told the operator. "See if you can find Markey. Call me." He dropped the phone on its cradle and got out of his chair and sat on the edge of his desk. "See what names we've got and get pictures," he told Rausch. "Try for some cuts, too."

The phone rang and he scooped it up. It was Harry Markey, circulation manager.

"We got a Paris plane lost," he said. "Good names it looks like. How are you fixed?"

"I can give you about fifteen minutes," said Markey. "No more than that. We can't blow those trains."

"O.K. I'll have a replate for you."

Crowell kept the phone to his ear and jiggled the bar. When the operator came on he said, "Get me Hazel right away.   Then call Mr. Polk at his home and put him on as soon as you get him.   Break in on any call I'm making."

"Will do," said the operator cheerily.   She was Mabel Garth, and she had been on the *Press* switchboard for twenty years, her life devoted to the people of the newspaper and their daily crises.   She knew as well as Sam Crowell or George Hazel, the composing room foreman, or William Barr Polk, the general manager, what was to be done and who should do it.

Sam Crowell talked briefly to George Hazel.   He told him that a replate was coming and they would need some two columns of type in a hurry, plus new headlines for page one. Then the call from Bill Polk came through, and Mabel cut off this conversation.

"Mr. Polk?" said Sam.   "Sorry to bother you this early. This is Sam Crowell.   We've got a lost airliner—Paris plane out of Idlewild.   Some good names on board.   We ought to have a couple more pages."

"Have you talked to Mr. Victory?" demanded Mr. Polk. He was annoyed, not so much at being awakened at this hour as by his general distaste for editorial department employees, whom he considered extravagant, worthless and drunkards. Mr. Polk had come to New York only two years before from Kansas City.   He had been dismayed at the easy camaraderie he had found on the *Press*—not at all like the *Bulletin* back home—and he had refused to become a part of it.

"Why should I bother Judd Victory?" said Sam.   "We've got 115 columns today.   That's too tight with a big story running.   It's seven columns under our budget.   I want two more pages."

"You tell Mr. Victory what you want, young man," said William Barr Polk.   "Have Mr. Victory call me if he wishes."

He hung up the telephone and scratched his chest under his blue-striped silk pajamas with satisfaction.   He poured a glass of water from the silver-plated carafe on the bedside table and then selected a brown bottle from the array of pill vials on the table. He uncorked it, shook out a small pink pill into the palm of his hand, popped it into his mouth, then sipped the water. He stretched out in the double bed, his left foot resting against the calf of Mrs. Polk's big leg, waiting for the phone to ring again.

Sam Crowell phoned Judd Victory, managing editor of the *Press*.

"Sorry to bother you, boss," he said. "Oceanic's lost one of their Paris planes. Some good names on board. Greta Fortune's one of them. Dr. Finstone's another. Forty-eight in all. We need two more pages. I just called William Barr Polk and he told me to talk to you. He wants the request to come through you."

"That sanctimonious little twerp," said Victory, with no particular emphasis. "Well, all right. How many columns we got?"

"Hundred and fifteen, boss. She's as tight as an Armenian pawnbroker."

"O.K. I'll get an A and B page to go ahead of two and three. Get a lot of pictures. I'll be down in an hour. Maybe sooner."

Crowell hung up the phone, grinned at it briefly, then called George Hazel again. "We're going up two," he said. "Tell the pressroom, will you, George? I'll give you a second replate as soon as we get in with the flash."

"Two pages?" exclaimed George Hazel. "Are you out of your fat mind? My crew goes off in half an hour. You *know* that."

"You've got to fill two pages, so you figure out how to do it," said Sam.

"It'll mean overtime," wailed the foreman.

"Sure it will, chum. And I bet you catch hell from William Barr Polk."

Crowell cradled the phone and walked over to the city desk, reading over Lew Hanford's shoulder the story of the missing airliner, paragraph by paragraph, as it came from the typewriter of Hal Foster.

Hal had a definite flair for writing such news stories under pressure. He was a master of the simple, declarative sentence, and he kept the paragraphs short and easily digestible. He eschewed adjectives and modifying clauses, giving color with active and unusual verbs. He kept a list of these verbs with him in a small notebook at all times, adding to them whenever he ran across new ones. "I've got a verb fetish," he would tell those who commented upon his writing. "I inherited it from my father, who was a top sergeant."

Crowell called over to Frank Goodman, head of the copy desk. "Set it all in two-twelve," he said. "Put Foster's by-line on it."

The night editor then moved to Phil Rausch's desk as Carl Yerbe brought a dozen large envelopes filled with pictures and zinc engravings. Rausch spread out all of the cuts of Greta Fortune, alone and with her husband, and together they selected a three-column cut of the two of them, taken a few months before at the Academy Award dinner in Hollywood.

"We'll use this on page one," said Crowell. "See if you have one-columns of Finstone and his wife and Lamar Hinemann. Get 'em all blocked. I'll be in the composing room."

Within ten minutes a new page one was being justified by Luke Appling, page one makeup man. There were two lines of 120-point gothic reading:

N.Y.-PARIS PLANE LOST;
GRETA FORTUNE ABOARD

The story occupied the last two columns of the page, and next to it was the three-column cut of Greta and Mark Cassell, smiling for the photographer, their shoulders touching. Under this were one-column cuts of Harvey Finstone, Laura Finstone and Lamar Hinemann.

Appling locked up the page form with the screws on side and bottom, then shoved it off the steel table onto a metal truck held by a composing room apprentice. The boy pushed the truck to the stereotype table in the rear of the room, and big Ed Healey, stereotype foreman, took over. He slid the form off the truck, pounded down the type with a wood planer and mallet, then placed a matrix and blankets on top of the page. He pressed a black button on the control beside the huge steel roller, and the page form went slowly under the roller with its thousands of pounds of pressure.

Blankets and matrix were removed at the other side. The matrix was trimmed and packed and put on a conveyor to the foundry, on the mezzanine floor of the pressroom. Jim Coster took it off the conveyor and popped in into the drier. In one minute the matrix popped out of the machine like a piece of toast. Coster placed it in the casting machine and pressed a button, and in twenty seconds a metal plate the size of the newspaper page, cast in a semi-circle to fit on the press, emerged from the casting machine. Coster lifted it with asbestos pads on his hands to the conveyor to the pressroom and pressed a red button beside the conveyor. A bell started to ring. In thirty seconds more the first press started slowly, gaining speed and filling the vaulted room with its thunder.

Bill Frischetti, pressroom foreman, handed the first paper off the press to Harry Markey, standing at his side. Markey looked at the first page with a scowl, then slapped the page with the back of his hand. The circulation man yelled his criticism, unheard over the roar of the press, to Frischetti, then hurried to his office at the other end of the building on the floor above.

He burst into the office and put the paper in front of Morrie Suskind, country and suburban circulation manager. "Look at that," he exclaimed. "Them knuckleheads got Greta Fortune and they ain't got sense enough to run a picture of her legs! How the hell they expect me to sell papers?"

CHAPTER TWO

PETE MOREHOUSE was wide-awake before the telephone had ended its first ring. He plucked it out of its cradle on the table beside the bed, swung his feet to the floor, turned on the bedside lamp, and picked up a pencil, almost in one motion.

"Pete Morehouse," he said into the phone.

"Hello, Mr. Morehouse. This is Mabel. I thought you'd want to know. An Oceanic Airways plane is missing over the Atlantic. Lots of big names aboard. One of them is Greta Fortune. They've just replated. They're going up two pages."

"Thanks, Mabel," said Pete. "I'll be in as soon as I can make it."

"O.K., Pete. Good-bye."

Pete sat on the bed for a moment looking at the phone. Cissie reached out a hand and touched his shoulder. "What is it, Pete?" she asked.

"Oceanic plane down in the Atlantic," he said. He turned and looked at her in the dim light of the reading lamp. Cissie was resting on an elbow, her head against the backboard of the bed. Her short hair looked unaccountably neat, and her body had all of the curves of youth despite her forty-three years. He smiled at her because he liked her.

"Gosh," she said. "Who's on it?"

"Big shots," he said. "Those Oceanic planes carry only the best. One of 'em's Greta Fortune... Well, I'd better get going." He stood up and stretched.

"Greta Fortune," exclaimed Cissie. "What a story. That's like—you remember Carole Lombard?"

"Sure. Same thing. We'll go to town on this one."

"Yes, *we'll* go to town," she echoed. It was a bitter echo.

Pete had started for the bathroom. He turned and came back to the bed, sat on the edge and reached out a hand to his wife.

"Look, Cissie, don't feel that way. It's all right. It doesn't bother me a bit."

"No, it doesn't bother *you*. The great Pete Morehouse, keeper of the morgue."

He shook his head slowly, looking down at his feet. "Don't rub it in, honey," he said mildly.

"I'm sorry," she replied. "You know that I'm always nasty when I first wake up."

"It's a job," he said, "and a pretty good job. Only five days a week and my own staff and my own office. I'm the boss. What I say goes... You know, they couldn't get anywhere without me. They couldn't get out a paper without my library, without my clippings and my pictures. There just wouldn't be any paper."

"I'm sorry," she said again.

"Running a big metropolitan newspaper morgue is nothing to be ashamed of," he continued. "You've really got to know your stuff—and I do. I know where everything in that place is—every single thing. Only yesterday Colonel Gaylord himself called and asked me to get him the dates of the Anzio landings... He called me Pete."

"Sure, honey," she said. "You'd better get dressed. You've got a long ride into the city."

"I'm not young enough now for that other stuff," he said, determined to make himself clear. "Wouldn't I look silly chasing fire engines at my age?"

"You never chased fire engines... Get dressed, will you, Pete? Get out of here and let me get some sleep."

He got up and started again for the bathroom. At the door he turned and looked back at Cissie.

"All of this newspaper reporter stuff is for kids," he said. "Sure, I wanted to be a great reporter once—and I guess I was pretty good. Then I got sidetracked and went on the city desk. That was a mistake. I should have stayed out on the street. I shouldn't have let them make me a clerk, but I did, and I've got no one to blame but myself. So I'm a clerk. I'm not a reporter."

"You could be a reporter again any time you wanted," said Cissie. She had heard this a thousand times, and she had her answer ready. It was like a play that had been running for years.

"Yeah. I could go to the *Telegram* or the *Journal* or the *News*—for a twenty-five-dollar cut. No thanks."

"Well, leave it alone then," said Cissie, suddenly deviating from the lines of the script. "You're flogging the subject to death." What she usually said, what she should have said, was: "You're right, honey. You can't take a cut."

In an immense penthouse apartment on Sutton Place, overlooking the East River, the telephone rang in a bedroom of crystal and satin. The arm that reached for the telephone on its second ring was slender and firm, and the fingers that grasped the instrument were beautifully tapering and tipped with silvered nails. The voice that answered was throaty, yet cultured—a sexy voice.

"Hello," said Judy Starr Hinemann.

"The plane is down," said a man's voice. "It's on the radio."

Judy Starr Hinemann jerked the phone away from her ear as though it had burned her. She looked at the instrument for a moment, her heart pounding with fear.

She banged the telephone into its cradle and turned on the reading light over the bed. She clicked on the clock radio on the shelf behind the tufted satin headboard, then drew her knees up to her chin and encircled them with her beautiful arms. She listened to the rock 'n' roll coming from the radio, trying to concentrate on it, fighting to keep her thoughts away from the telephone and the airplane and, most of all, Lamar Hinemann.

She sat that way for nearly twenty minutes until the 5:30 news broadcast, listening to the records and the announcer's comments in between, humming the tunes and singing along with those whose lyrics she knew.

Then the news broadcast came on. "It has been definitely established that our own Greta Fortune is among the passengers on the missing Oceanic Airway plane, believed to be down in the Atlantic with forty-eight passengers. Miss Fortune and her husband, Mark Cassell, the noted writer and producer, boarded the Paris airliner at Idlewild—"

Judy Starr Hinemann clicked off the radio. She jumped out of bed and went into her pink bathroom. She took two large red pills from a bottle in the cabinet and downed them with a glass of water. She returned to her bed, turned off the light, and lay down with her knees against her breast and her head bowed, in the fetal position. She was unconscious within two minutes.

It had been snowing since midnight, a soft, wet snow that melted quickly as it hit the sidewalks and streets but collected in fluffy piles on ledges and in out-of-the-way corners. It left a deep slush that soaked the shoes of the few pedestrians abroad in the early hours of Friday.

One of these was Willard Gower, a partner in the firm of Erhardt and Gower, Radio & Television Service Repairs, 116½ Nassau Street, New York. He was a small, disheveled man in his mid-forties, a navy veteran of World War II and Korea. He had learned his electronic art and a variety of other skills aboard navy repair ships, and his ability to diagnose and set to rights the infinitely complicated ailments of mechanical organisms amounted to genius. But his careful and reverent handling of tools and pieces of machinery could not disguise the fact that he was a very ordinary and unprepossessing figure, his clothes shabby, his nails black, his sparse hair uncombed, his face almost always needing a shave.

Willard Gower locked the front door of Erhardt & Gower at 6:07 A.M. and stood with his back to the door gazing malevolently at the snow. He looked down for a moment at his worn, inadequate shoes. Already he could feel the cold wetness oozing through the hole in his right sole. That reminded him of the state of his finances, and he put his hand in his right pocket and felt the single banknote there. He could buy all the shoes he wanted, now. He looked up and down the street to make certain he was alone. It was a frightened look.

He turned north on Nassau Street and hurried along through the slush to the Chambers Street subway entrance, his shabby tweed overcoat buttoned high around his neck and his greasy felt pulled down over his eyes. He scurried with furtive glances at the half dozen other people abroad at this hour, like a mouse in flight. And like a mouse he ducked down into the hole of the subway. It seemed that Willard Gower was running from someone or something.

A train had just pulled out and the platform seemed empty. He looked quickly up and down the platform, then hurried behind the stairway, where he would not be observed by those descending, and stood with his back to the wall. His feet were wet now, cold and uncomfortable, and his fingers tightly clasped the single bill in his pocket. He thought about the money, but since he was not an avaricious man, it did not give him much pleasure. Not nearly as much as he had expected.

The two men had been standing behind the change booth, silent and watchful. They could see all who entered the turnstiles, though it was unlikely they would have been noticed by anyone entering the subway. Dark complexioned, of medium height and dressed in dark overcoats and grey hats, they looked pretty much alike, at a quick glance.

They saw Willard scurry through the gate and start down the stairs. They looked at each other briefly, then sauntered through the turnstile and followed him.

They seemed to know where to find him. Splitting up at the bottom of the stairs, they approached his place from either side of the wall. They didn't look at him or at each other. They stood at each corner of the wall, their backs to each other and to Willard.

Willard saw them the moment they stopped. He swiveled his head from one to the other, and there was new fear in his eyes. He took his right hand out of his pocket and balanced on his toes as though he were going to start running. But neither man made a move toward him or even looked at him, so he settled back again, put his hand back on the money and continued to look from one man to the other.

The rumble of the train could be heard far up the tunnel. It grew louder very slowly. Willard waited nearly a minute, then started to walk to the rear of the platform. He could see the lights up the track, one red and one green, which meant that his train to Brooklyn was approaching.

The rumble had grown to a roar as he stood near the platform's edge. His mind completely on the train, he had forgotten to be scared and watchful. The two men came up behind him fast, and suddenly Willard felt himself propelled through the air. His mouth opened wide and he screamed, a wild, piercing animal scream. It was not heard over the roar of the train, now entering the station, except by the two dark-complexioned men.

Willard landed on the tracks ten feet in front of the train, and his scream was almost immediately cut off. The only sound that anyone heard then was the metallic screech of the train's brakes as the motorman brought it to the quickest possible halt and the panicky *bleet* of the air whistle as the motorman signaled an emergency.

It was 6:38 A.M. when Carl Yerbe, *New York Press* office boy, dropped his token into the slot at the Chambers Street subway station, banged through and started to run for the stairs. He heard the train as it rumbled into the station, then the screech of the brakes and the cry of the whistle. He didn't attach any importance to this until he reached the top of the stairway and saw that the train had stopped with its first car less than halfway down the platform.

He paused momentarily at the top of the steps to regard this phenomenon and he saw the two dark-coated, grey-hatted men running up the stairs side by side. They passed him without a glance and slammed through the turnstiles together. He didn't turn to look at them. He heard the noise of the turnstiles as he continued down the stairway.

The motorman and the conductor of the train were coming out of the rear door of the first car. The motorman's face was white, and he grimaced as though he were in pain.

Then he whirled suddenly and put his head down between the two cars and retched.

"What happened?" asked Carl Yerbe.

The conductor looked at him blankly, then started to push past him.

"I'm from the *Press*. I'm a reporter," said Yerbe. "You got to tell me what happened."

"We ran over a man," said the conductor over his shoulder as he hurried to the stairway.

Yerbe turned and looked at the motorman's heaving back, then followed the conductor up the stairs. He met two policemen and the station agent coming down.

"Somebody just got run over!" he yelled at them.

The three looked at Yerbe curiously but said nothing. They continued down and Yerbe ran up to a pay telephone near the change booth that was now closed.

He dropped a dime in the slot and dialed the number of the *Press* with a nervous finger. Mabel Garth said, "*New York Press*. Good morning."

"This is Carl Yerbe," he said, forcing his voice down to a normal pitch. "Give me Mr. Hanford right away, please. There's been an accident."

"Sure enough," said Mabel.

Almost instantly he heard Lew Hanford's voice, "City desk."

"This is Carl Yerbe. I'm at the Chambers Street I.R.T. subway station. A man's just been run over by a train. Downtown side."

"Well?"

"Well… That's all. He was run over."

"What's his name?"

"I don't know, I… The conductor just told me."

"Jesus Christ! Here we've got the biggest story of the year breaking all over the place, and you call me up to tell me that? Why you little nuisance…"

The phone crashed in his ear. Yerbe looked at his receiver for a moment, then placed it gently on the hook. He opened the door of the booth and started to go back down to the platform, but he discovered that he didn't have another token to get through the turnstile. And the change booth was closed. So he leaned against the turnstile and waited for the attendant to come back.

Francine Addams was in the small, untidy bathroom washing her teeth when the telephone rang. With the first sound of the bell she knew it was for her. She knew it was the office, too. At least she knew she *had* known these things when she got to the bedroom in response to Lori's call and found that she was *right*. It was the office. It was Lew Hanford.

"Fran?" he said. "Look, honey, get over to 22 Sutton Place South in about an hour, and get in to see a dame by the name of Judith Starr Hinemann. Mrs. Lamar Hinemann. Got that? You know who he is. She's got penthouse D. Get to see her one way or another. Don't take no for an answer. She's going to be all broken up, so you've got to use finesse. Hinemann was a passenger on the Oceanic airliner that's missing."

"Wait a minute," said Fran, "catch me up. *What* airliner is missing?"

"Where the hell have you been, girl? The V.I.P. flight to Paris, with Greta Fortune aboard. It's probably down in the drink. Don't you know what's going on?"

"Only what's been going on in my beddie-bye, and that's been me, sleeping. Look, tough guy, I was up until two A.M.

at that damned Animal Ball at the Waldorf, and I know from nothing."

"O.K., let's start all over again. It's a brand new day. You've got an assignment. It's to interview the probable and potential widow of Lamar Hinemann, the financier, who has been lost in an airplane accident. Got that?"

"You're the nastiest genius on the city desk," said Fran. "However, I forgive you. I'll be there."

"O.K. I'm sending Les Howard. He'll meet you in the lobby."

"Good-bye, darling," said Fran.

"What's that all about?" asked Lori Vale, sitting up in the other twin bed and lighting a cigarette.

"They lost an airplane with a lot of important people aboard," said Fran, lying back on her own bed. "Greta Fortune was one, Lamar Hinemann was another."

"Lamar Hinemann?"

"A friend of yours?"

"No. But I used to know him."

"What about him?"

"He's a pig, honey."

"How about Mrs. Lamar Hinemann?"

"Judy? She's all right, I guess."

"You guess? What's wrong with her?"

"Nothing much, except that she married Lamar... She must have been awfully hungry."

"But you went around with him."

"Sure. But I didn't *marry* him."

"Where'd you know this Judy?"

"At the Gay Paree. I worked there nearly a year before I got this television job."

"You never told me about that, darling."

"No, I never did. And I never told you about Lamar or a

lot of other johns either. What would you like to know, now that I'm taking my hair down?"

"Just about Judy. How'll I get in to see her?"

"You won't. She's cut everybody since her marriage. She can't distinguish me from a knothole in the woodwork."

"I've got to get an interview with her. It's my job."

Lori shook her blonde head and crushed out her cigarette in the ashtray on the nightstand. "She's an odd girl, Frannie. She doesn't think the way we do—the way normal people do. She was friendly enough with me and the other girls, but it was only on the surface. She was always holding something back. You never got to know the real Judy Starr, if there was one. All you got to know was this superficial and pleasant little female who didn't seem to have a care in the world or a thought in her head. But she did have thoughts, plenty of them. And deep down I always suspected that she was as rock-hard and as calculating as an abacus...I think that she knew exactly what she was doing when she married Hinemann."

"So, where do I fit in?" demanded Fran.

"Look. Send a note up to her. Tell her you know a lot about her that you've been talking to me. Tell her you think you can help her."

"She doesn't need any help, with all that Hinemann dough," said Fran, jumping up from the bed and starting to dress.

"I think she's in trouble," insisted Lori. "I have a feeling..."

CHAPTER THREE

BY SATURDAY, December 7, there wasn't a gram of doubt left that the missing Flight 900 of Oceanic Airways had fallen into the Atlantic and was lost forever. No wreckage yet had been found by the scores of planes and vessels that searched the empty seascape in the area of 40 West on the airliner's last reported course—no lifeboats and no bodies. The search was being pushed to the utmost by the navy, coast guard and air force, as well as by Oceanic Airlines. No square yard of the ocean was being left unexamined for some 200 miles east of 40 West and twenty miles on each side of the airliner's known course.

High up in the tower of the Oceanic Airlines Building on Park Avenue, Willis Harrington, president of the airline, paced behind his huge bleached-mahogany desk and spoke haltingly but with great sincerity to the men ranged in chairs facing the desk. He was a huge bear of a man, well over six feet tall and 210 pounds, very little of it fat. Despite grey hair, he looked younger than his fifty-three years. Now his thick hair curled, disheveled, down over his wide forehead, as though he had just climbed out of bed. But there was nothing sleepy about his deep blue eyes, and there was nothing indecisive about his mouth, despite the slowness of his speech. The slowness was a habit that he had acquired early in Virginia.

"Our safety record for the past several years is no accidental thing," he said. "We know how to run an airline, and we know how to keep our planes out of accidents... Such an affair as this is intolerable, and I'm not going to accept it as an accident and tell myself, 'Better luck next time.' I tell you that plane was sabotaged somewhere along the line. We're working on that. We're spending twenty-four hours a day working on that. And I think it's about time we got some cooperation from some of you gentlemen. That's what I wanted to say."

He sat down abruptly at his desk and leaned back in the large swivel chair, looking from one to the other of his listeners. They were a distinguished company: Calvin C.

Colby, Special Agent In Charge of the New York office, FBI; Walter Cross, chief investigator for the C.A.B.; Dr. Carleton Beall Gideon, representing the North American Airlines Association; Foster Logan, chief engineer of Northeast Aircraft (builder of the lost Triton airliner); Gordon Buell, first deputy police commissioner of New York; and Cameron Hawkes, vice president of Oceanic in charge of advertising and public relations.

The six remained silent. FBI agent Colby took a small leather-bound notebook from his pocket and wrote in it. Foster Logan lit a cigarette. Dr. Gideon uncrossed his legs and scratched his ankle. The other three sat unmoving and watchful.

Willis Harrington picked up several sheets of paper stapled together. "This is the passenger list of Flight 900," he said. "I want you to listen to some of this. Cameron Hawkes here dug it up for us. It's the kind of stuff that's available to anyone... Now here's this Dr. Harvey Finstone, director of International Charities. You know what this I.C.A. is, Mr. Colby? It's a racket. The sole purpose of the I.C.A. is to make money for Finstone and such people as Duke Haywood, Filmore Hyde, Howard Morescou and Louis Balthazar. I am sure these four names are familiar to Mr. Colby and Mr. Buell. They've all got records. Harvey Finstone is their front man, but it's these four who own the I.C.A.... So maybe they wanted to get rid of their front man, and what would be simpler than to put a bomb in his luggage and dump him and our plane into the ocean?

"Here's another, Clarence Maiden, president of the Amalgamated Chauffeurs and Drivers, on his way to the International Labor Conference at Brussels. I don't have to tell you about the A.C.D. and Maiden. Only six months ago Maiden's home at Stony Point was bombed, and he came out of it with a left arm that's been useless since. Two years ago he was shot from ambush up in the Bronx—you worked on that didn't you, Mr. Buell? Well, do you think the boys have given up trying to get Mr. Maiden?

"Down here we've got another one of interest, Aldo Vincenzi. Cameron Hawkes tells me Mr. Vincenzi was among those present at the November meeting of the syndicate at Little Falls. What do you think about a member of the crime syndicate on one of our planes that disappeared? Wouldn't that be worth investigating?

"So much for the criminal element. We have some fat prospects to look into there. But let's look back over a couple of airplane accidents wherein sabotage was established. There was the Denver plane—the one where the vicious young Jack Graham put a time bomb in mama's baggage so he could collect the insurance on her life. Graham was not in the class of Finstone's gang or Maiden or Vincenzi, nor was it known beforehand that he was particularly vicious. This came out later. Then there is the Canadian sabotage case of some years ago. A husband wanted to get rid of his wife so he could marry another girl, and he sent a whole planeload of innocent people to their deaths to do it. He wasn't a criminal either—until he committed this crime of mass murder. What I'm trying to get at is that I think we should also look for another Graham or someone like this Canadian Lothario behind the loss of our plane.

"Most people are worth more dead than alive, from the standpoint of actual cash. And there's always somebody that's going to benefit. Just look at some of the people who were on Flight 900: Franklyn Petrie and his wife, who is the Crescent Ale heiress; Henry Doble of Pierce, Doble and Samson; Walter Begley of Fountain Steel; Hanna Prentice who owns more than a half a million shares of Monarch Motors; Martha Faulkner, who controls Hamilton Freres; the

Baron Otto Vitell, who's supposed to run the Orient-East oil trust; Aristotle Coulardis, the shipping magnate; Lamar Hinemann, who's one of the richest men in the world today; and last but not least, Winchell Manson, the playboy financier who got control of Pacific and Western last month in that noisy proxy battle.

"What is it worth to the survivors to have anyone of these people dead? I won't belabor the point. What I want to say is that someone blew up our plane to get rid of one of the passengers—one of these or one of the others."

Willis Harrington fell silent. He leaned back in his chair and closed his eyes, waiting for someone else to speak. Dr. Gideon of the National Airlines Association said, "There isn't much to go on, Willis. You're voicing a suspicion that I suppose we all entertain, but it's a very thin suspicion at this time."

"It isn't thin," declared Harrington, opening his eyes and looking at the bland face of Dr. Gideon. "There's no doubt at all that that plane blew up; otherwise we would have heard the contrary from Captain Lochman or one of the other members of the crew. I'll tell you what happened, Carl. A time bomb in the forward baggage compartment went off right after Lochman's report from 40 West. The explosion severed all of the power lines to the cockpit, as an explosion in that compartment could easily do, and the radios went out. That's why we didn't hear from them."

"It's too thin, Willis," insisted Dr. Gideon.

"But it's possible and not unlikely," said Foster Logan, chief engineer of Northeast Aircraft, who had been one of the designers of the Triton airliners. "Both main and emergency power lines pass through the forward baggage compartment... Of course, there could be other causes of power failure."

"Exactly," said Dr. Gideon.

"We can't do anything until we can examine some of the wreckage," said Walter Cross of the C.A.B. "If we find evidence of an explosion, then of course we shall request the FBI to investigate."

"What do you say, Mr. Colby?" asked Willis Harrington.

"I agree with Mr. Cross," he said. "However, we are now inquiring into two of your passengers, Clarence Maiden and Aldo Vincenzi, although not necessarily with sabotage in view."

"Well, that's something," said Harrington with a slight smile.

You were likely to find Pete Morehouse in the *Press* morgue at any hour of the day or night. There were several reasons for this. One was that he was genuinely conscientious, if there was any slightest possibility that a breaking story would require unusual background material or any of the special knowledge he possessed of where to find cuts and pictures and references, he would prefer to remain in his dusty office on the floor below the editorial room to make certain these needs were fulfilled. Another reason was that his affection for the *Press* was deep and sincere—that this newspaper was, in fact, the most important reality, and that everything else in his life came after it—even Cissie. Pete had started on the *Press* as an office boy in 1923, and he had never known any other employment in his adult life.

At 10:00 P.M. on the Saturday after the loss of Flight 900, Pete was still in his office. He was going through the last of the day's clippings, which were to be filled, and he was talking to Carl Yerbe, the office boy, who worked the 8:00 to 4:00 A.M. trick Saturday for the Sunday *Press* and was on his lunch hour. Yerbe had asked and had been granted permission to go through the clipping file in search of a person he said he was interested in. He returned to Pete's office empty-handed and sad-eyed.

"What's the trouble?" Pete asked. He was one of the few on the *Press* who would bother to inquire into the problems of an office boy.

"It's this accident I saw last night," Yerbe replied. "I just can't get over that guy. You know, he had a thousand dollar bill in his pocket…"

Pete laid a handful of clippings on his desk and tilted back in his chair. "You run into that kind of thing all the time in New York," he said. "Bums—frowsy old men and women who rake over the garbage cans for their food—and then they die somehow, and the police find thousands of dollars stashed away in their hovels. You shouldn't let it bother you."

"This guy was different," said Yerbe. "He wasn't a bum; he was one of the owners of this television and radio shop down on Nassau Street. Name of Willard Gower."

"Gower," repeated Pete. "Let me see—I was just reading that clipping." He sorted through a stack of small envelopes in a basket on his desk and pulled one out. "Here it is." He took out the clipping and read it.

"*Willard H. Gower, forty-three years old, of 1537 Sterling Place, Brooklyn—'* hmmm…*'fell or jumped…two men seen with him just before the accident by the motor-man.'* Here's something. Did you read this in the *Times? 'Mrs. Gower told police that her husband had seemed nervous and depressed for the past several days and did not come home last night. He telephoned her at eleven P.M. and told her he was going to meet some men and collect some money they owed him. He would not tell her anything more, she said, and when she tried to question him he said merely, "Oh, it's a lot. You'll see." Then he had hung up. She could not account in any other way for the thousand-dollar bill found in Mr. Gower's pocket. She said she had never seen a thousand-dollar bill in her life and that her husband never carried such a sum. "We are not wealthy people," she said."*

"I read all that," said Yerbe.

"Well, what are you trying to find out?"

"Who he was. I don't mean his name and all that, but, well, where he came from and if he's ever been in the papers before."

"You just trying to satisfy your personal curiosity?" Pete asked.

"Well, I think there's a story. There ought to be a story. Besides there were those two men who were with him. I saw them. Maybe they pushed him."

"We've got a good story running right now," said Pete, putting the clipping back into the envelope. "That airplane is enough for one night."

Fran Addams came into the library carrying coffee and a sandwich and sat in the chair Yerbe vacated, putting her food on a corner of Pete's desk.

"You didn't tell me," she said.

Pete looked at her and shook his head. Fran was a brown-eyed brunette with a beautiful figure that she disguised with loose tweeds in the winter. She had a minimum of interest in clothes and her personal appearance, which is not uncommon among the newspaper sisterhood. Fran spent all of her effort being a newspaperwoman and cheerfully relinquished most of the time-consuming vanities of her sex unless there was a good reason.

"It wasn't much of a story," Pete replied, his gentle tone taking the sting out of his words. "Seems to me you could have done better than that with the prospective widow of Lamar Hinemann."

When Fran Addams had first started on the *Press*, Pete Morehouse had been on the city desk, and it was he who had given her her first assignments and had read and criticized her copy. In fact it was Pete alone who had been largely responsible for her development into a sound reporter and a fair writer, occasionally revealing brilliance. He had taught her with patience and firmness; he had insisted that she be thorough and tireless in accumulating her facts and logical in her presentation of them.

"That girl has me stumped," said Fran, taking the top off her coffee container. "There wasn't anything to write about her—that a newspaper would print."

"Where'd you get that stuff on her background?" asked Pete. "I didn't see that anywhere else."

"My roommate, Lori Vale, used to be with her at the Gay Paree. I got some of it from her, and then when I finally got in to see her, I had something to talk about, and she opened up a little—just a little. The important things, she wouldn't tell me, such as where she was born and who her parents were, and where she went to school."

Pete went to a rack behind his desk and got a Saturday *Press*. "Let me read you something," he said, sitting down and opening the paper. *"'The small, delicate blonde girl—she looked to be no more than twenty—sat in the corner of the huge divan, her feet curled under her, and spoke haltingly, almost incoherently, of her husband. The man she spoke of was Lamar Hinemann, one of the richest men in the world, and the girl who spoke was his wife, Judy Starr Hinemann, who may become the wealthiest widow in the world…'"*

"Well?" said Fran.

"Not very well," said Pete. "Isn't there one single thing she said that would have made a lead for you? I can't believe it. Over here on the jump—" he turned the page—"you quote her saying, *It was a business trip. He was to have been gone only a few weeks. Also he was going to stop off at Liege to receive a doctorate of laws—he had done a lot for the Belgians after the war. Yes, I had refused to go with him. I'm afraid of airplanes. I didn't want him to fly either, but he would never listen to me.'* What's the matter with that for a lead, Fran?"

She took a sip of coffee to wash down a mouthful of sandwich. She shook her head. "That isn't what she actually said, Pete. What she said was, 'He's got some floozie in Paris and he flew over to see her whenever he got the urge. I know all about her—in fact he made no secret of it. He was that kind of guy. I told him I hoped the plane would fall in the ocean. So maybe it has.'"

Pete looked at Fran for a long time and didn't say anything. She ate her sandwich and drank her coffee. Then she said, "I'd rather be me with this job and never any money than Judy Hinemann with all her millions. The price is too high, Pete. You know what she told me? This Hinemann would have girls and men in for all sorts of exhibitions and parties. Sometimes he would force her to participate. He would beat her unmercifully if she refused. What miserable people…"

"That's a high, moral tone you're taking," said Pete.

"I'm not talking about the immorality at all," declared Fran. "It's just that a girl like this Judy would allow herself to be so degraded… She's an awfully attractive girl, Pete. Really beautiful."

"She's been well paid, just like all of the others," he replied. "Let me tell you, Fran, that the longer you're in this newspaper business, the less respect you're going to have for your fellow human beings. People call us cynics—they criticize us for being hard boiled and unromantic and materialistic. How the hell else can you be when you see people as they actually are, day after day? When you have to watch them practicing their meanness and their vices and their animal ugliness. All of them. Not just a few here and there but all of them?"

"All of them but thee and me," she said.

"Well—yes. You're all right. You've got an unusual and a rare quality—you can get down into the gutter with the lowest of them and nothing touches you, none of the filth and nastiness. I wish the hell you'd get out of this business though, and get married and raise a family, as you should."

"And stop messing around in your man's world," she said. "Well, maybe I will one day, if I can find me a man I can respect."

"There are plenty of them," said Pete. "You shouldn't have any trouble there."

"You talk out of both sides of your mouth. Didn't you just say nobody was any good—that the whole world is mean and vicious?"

"Not the man you'll marry," he said, smiling at her.

CHAPTER FOUR

ON MONDAY, December 9, the first bits of wreckage from Oceanic's Flight 900 of December 5 were found floating in the ocean some sixty miles east of the point 40 West. The wreckage included a section of wing that floated because of its honeycomb construction and the air trapped inside; two seats buoyed up by the air cushions used in Northeast aircraft; several pieces of baggage; several pillows; some life jackets; a lady's pocketbook; and a number of pieces of paper. The discovery was made by the coast guard cutter *Vincennes* and the information radioed immediately to the C.A.B. Within minutes the story was on the A.P. and U.P. wires into the office of the *New York Press*.

The story broke at 1:37 P.M., and a replate on page one was ordered immediately by Judd Victory, managing editor. Within fifteen minutes the presses were spewing out papers with the double headline:

FIND WRECKAGE OF PARIS
PLANE, MISSING WITH 48

The story was written by George Houseman, under his byline from the A.P. and U.P. wires and from the clips. It was largely a re-hash of the stories of the previous days, stressing once again the prominent names of the passenger list, with the glamorous Greta Fortune leading them all. In addition to this lead story on page one, there was the life story of Greta, which had started in the Sunday paper, written especially for the *Press* by Lorraine Gates, Hollywood columnist.

Houseman's story was a workmanlike job, giving the *Press* readers once again all of the facts that were known about the airliner and its passengers and crew. Toward the middle of the story there was one brief paragraph, entirely new that had been contributed by Pete Morehouse. When Houseman had telephoned the morgue for the clippings, he had got Pete on the phone and had told him briefly that the first wreckage of the plane had been found.

"That's it, then," Pete had said. "I'll give you something you might want to put in your story. I was talking to Cameron Hawkes this morning—he wanted me to lend him some background material on the passengers—and he told me they believe the plane was sabotaged and that Oceanic has demanded an investigation by the FBI."

"That's a hell of a lead," said Houseman. "Is it safe to use?"

"Yeah, but not for the lead, for Christ sake. Put it down in the story somewhere or I'll get scalped by Hawkes."

"O.K."

Then Houseman had passed the information on to Finley Browne, city editor.

"Sure, they always cry sabotage when one of their fancy airplanes falls apart," Browne had said. "What would you expect them to say—that their planes are just no damned good? Use it down in the story, Pete Morehouse is reliable."

Houseman's paragraph read:

It was learned on reliable authority today that officials of Oceanic Airways have demanded an investigation of sabotage by the FBI. The Press learned exclusively that the airline officials believe that a time bomb was placed aboard the plane before it took off from Idlewild and that the plane was blown up by this means. Local officials of the FBI have refused to comment.

Browne didn't see the paragraph until the replate edition was going to press. He read it in the dupes and called Houseman angrily.

"What the hell's this?" he demanded. "You didn't say anything about a *time bomb*."

"No," admitted Houseman, "but if it was sabotage, there's no other kind of sabotage that would dump a plane in the ocean some four hours after it had taken off."

"Goddamn it, stick to the facts. You can't assume it was a time bomb. You can't assume anything. Take that out about the bomb. Get it corrected right away."

Houseman took the dupe from Browne's hand and ran out to the composing room to ask Judd Victory to make the correction. He told him of Browne's complaint and showed him the marked dupe.

"That's academic," said Judd, reading the dupe. "If it's sabotage, it might as well be a time bomb as anything else. And they'll never find out whether it was or wasn't with that plane at the bottom of the ocean. Leave it in. Leave it alone."

"O.K.," said Houseman dubiously, "but it's my neck."

On Monday afternoon Pete Morehouse telephoned Cissie at Floral Park and told her he would not be home until very late. This was no new thing to his wife, who had been calling herself a "newspaper widow" for more than twenty years.

"But I won't be at the office," Pete said. "I'm going to have dinner with Cameron Hawkes."

"You're going to get drunk with Cameron Hawkes, and then the pair of you are going to go out and chase floozies," said Cissie, without any bitterness.

"No, we're just going to have dinner," said Pete. "We might have a few drinks beforehand, but I know I'm not going to get drunk. I've got something else on my mind."

"That airplane accident," said Cissie. "Is that it?"

"Yes," said Pete, "that's it."

"Look, darling," she said, her voice suddenly becoming warm and sympathetic, "why don't you leave that sort of thing to the city desk and the reporters? Why butt your head against a stone wall?"

Pete sighed. "I don't know. I may be able to find out something they can't. I brought up Cam Hawkes in this business, and he'll tell me things he wouldn't tell to others... Well..."

"You'll never grow up, Pete," she said. "You'll never accept things as they are."

"I was a damn good reporter once and you know it," he said.

"All right, Pete, all right. Have fun."

"Good-bye, Cissie."

Pete met Cameron Hawkes at the bar in the Stork Club. He felt that he didn't belong in this place, this was not his milieu and these people around the bar and at the tables were not the kind of people he wanted to mingle with. He felt that he looked out of place—that he was attracting too much attention. But these were very vague feelings and didn't bother him much. When he was on the scent of a story, he would go anywhere and felt that he had a right to be there, whether or not he fitted in.

Cam Hawkes was sitting on a stool talking to one of the three bartenders when he came in. Hawkes looked as though he belonged. He had the clean, slick look of success. He was successful as newspapermen judged it. He earned at least $40,000 a year; he lived in a Park Avenue apartment, he associated with some of the best known names in business and the arts in New York. But Cam Hawkes had a right to all of this, too. His grandfather had been a governor of Virginia. His mother still did her yearly duty at Monticello. He had graduated from the University of Virginia and had attended the University of Paris for two years. Background. Pete didn't have any background except the *Press*. He had been born in Morristown, New Jersey, and he had come to New York to go to work. That's all.

"How are you, Cam?" he asked, walking up to him and putting a hand on his shoulder.

"Hello Pete," said Hawkes, turning and smiling. He had a lot of personality and charm, and when he smiled you felt that it had a special meaning for you.

"Let's go back in the Cub Room," he said. "I've got I table."

Pete followed the neatly groomed Hawkes to the rear room, aware that his own suit needed pressing and that his shoes could stand a shine. They sat side by side on a banquette and Hawkes ordered drinks—Scotch and soda for both.

"How's the *Press*?" he asked. "How's Vic and that old bastard Finley Browne?"

"They're O.K.," said Pete. "Nothing ever changes down there."

"No, I guess not," said Hawkes. He had had quite a few Scotches—at least five—and his speech was slightly thick. He moved his hands in a careless, clumsy way as he talked. "They gave you a bum deal, Pete, pushing you off in the morgue. I don't know why you take it."

"It's not so bad," said Pete. Their drinks arrived and he took a quick sip of his Scotch. "I still get my paycheck every week."

"Paycheck?" exclaimed Hawkes. "You're for sale too cheap, my boy."

"Look. Let's talk about this airliner," said Pete.

Hawkes gave him a long, appraising look, then sipped his drink. "O.K. What do you want to know?"

"About this sabotage. How do you figure that?"

"Elementary, my dear Morehouse. The captain reported normal flight in excellent weather. Then all of a sudden— nothing. He and his plane vanished. So it wasn't any usual emergency. It wasn't a busted fuel line or a couple of engines going out or anything at all that was wrong with the functioning of the plane. If it had been anything of that nature, the captain would have reported it. But he couldn't report what happened to his airplane because it was so sudden and so destructive that it was all over in an instant. Like an explosion. Like a bomb blast. You follow me?"

"Sure. That's possible."

"It's what happened," said Hawkes. "As soon as they examine the wreckage they found today, they'll confirm it."

"Everybody at Oceanic feel this way?" Pete asked.

"Yes, everybody. We know what we know."

"How about the FBI?"

"Are you going to pass any of this on?"

"No," said Pete, "it's strictly between us."

"O.K. The FBI is working on a couple of the passengers right now. Aldo Vincenzi is one. He's the crime syndicate mystery man. If they hadn't spotted him at that meeting at Little Falls, they'd never have connected him with the syndicate. He runs a legitimate travel agency, European-East Tours, and he owns the big yawl *Vesta IV* that finished third in last year's Bermuda race."

"What do you know," exclaimed Pete. "A yacht. Where'd you find that out?"

"I get around. Boat people do a lot of talking among themselves, and they know who owns what."

"The syndicate and a yacht," said Pete. "You know, Cam, that's a brand new angle. Yachts don't go through customs. They come and go as they please, and with an oceangoing job like the *Vesta* they could pick up one hell of a lot of heroin and dump it ashore here."

"Sure they could," agreed Hawkes. "They could send it over to Cuba or some other West Indian island and then the *Vesta* could bring it up here. All they'd need is some arrangement with ships that go to the West Indies."

"Like the ships of Aristotle Coulardis, another passenger on that plane."

"It's all very interesting," said Hawkes, "but it has nothing to do with the Triton that was dumped into the ocean. If the boys wanted to get rid of Vincenzi, it wouldn't have anything to do with the *Vesta IV*... As a matter of fact, I can't see this as a syndicate operation at all. They don't play that way. If they wanted Vincenzi dead, they wouldn't have to go to all this trouble. They've got too many journeymen executioners."

"Sure, sure, but that yacht angle would make one hell of a story... Well, it's not *this* story. Who else is the FBI interested in?"

"Clarence Maiden," said Hawkes. "Now don't get me wrong, Pete. This hasn't got anything to do with our airplane yet. The FBI has to have more evidence, but as soon as they analyze the wreckage they found today, they'll have their evidence. Of that we're all certain. *Then* watch the lid blow off."

"It's going to be a tremendous story, when and if it ever breaks," said Pete. "If they ever pin this on anyone, it's going to be the greatest murder story of the century. Greta Fortune, Baron Vitell, Aristotle Coulardis, Lamar Hinemann, Hanna Prentice, Winchell Manson—my God, what a jackpot."

"It's all of that," agreed Hawkes, "but strictly from the standpoint of airlines operations, it's poison. All of it. I've been dying for days now, trying to figure out how we can forget it—and make you muggs on the press forget it, too."

"That you'll never be able to do," said Pete. "So you might as well join us."

"Join Pete Morehouse, you mean, and give you all of the breaks."

"Sure, join me. What the hell's a friendship for if I can't impose on it?"

Hawkes finished his drink and ordered two more. He was deeply preoccupied for several minutes and Pete waited patiently for his answer. When the new drinks came, he took a large swallow.

"O.K." Pete," he said, "for old time's sake. But don't expect too much. The FBI isn't going to tell us any more than a minimum to keep Willis Harrington off their necks."

"Good enough," said Pete. "Now what do you say we order some dinner?"

The cutter *Vincennes* remained in the area where the first wreckage of the Oceanic plane was found for the next ten hours and picked up the bodies of three victims, as well as many more bits and pieces from the airliner. The bodies were those of Bettina Vincent, stewardess, Donald Walters, navigator, and Aristotle Coulardis.

Two days later the *Vincennes* came to the navy pier on the Hudson River with her cargo of tragedy, and the investigation into the loss of the airliner got properly under way. This investigation centered upon the pieces of metal and other debris picked up by the cutter. They were all taken to the FBI laboratory in Washington and subjected to a series of chemical tests.

On Thursday, December 12, at 3:47 P.M. Special Agent Calvin Colby telephoned Willis Harrington at the Oceanic Airlines offices. His report to Harrington was:

"There is positive evidence of a dynamite explosion. We have found traces of sodium nitrate, sodium carbonate, and several sulphur-bearing compounds on both the metal and the pieces of baggage. These are the chemical residues left by an explosion of dynamite. There is no question, Mr. Harrington, that your airplane was destroyed by a dynamite bomb."

"That verifies the suspicions of all of us here," said Harrington. "What are you going to do now, Mr. Colby?"

"We shall seek to find the person who placed the bomb aboard the airplane," he replied.

CHAPTER FIVE

IN OTHER TIMES, on another day, the arrest of the three men Luke Wardell, Morton Zannis and Louis Balthazar on charges of wiretapping (the technical charge was eavesdropping—violation of section 738 of the New York Penal Law) would have deserved and received better newspaper display than the three-quarters of a column on an inside page of the first afternoon edition of the *Press* of December 13.

The story had all the makings of a sensational incident in the financial affairs of the city, for the names of those whose telephones had been tapped in this conspiracy to steal stock market and business secrets (this was the police charge) were among the most prominent in the financial life of the city and the country. Not only that, but the three under arrest were very well known to newspaper readers.

Luke Wardell, an attorney, had handled many divorce and criminal cases of outstanding newspaper interest. He had defended Frankie LaBoue in the Madelaine Foster murder trial, thousands never forgave Wardell for getting Frankie off with a manslaughter conviction. He had defended Ruth Peyton and had won her an acquittal in the famous fire-tong slaying of her married lover, T. Jackson Cope. Only two years ago he had been the attorney for Winchell Manson in the latter's bitter—and very readable—courtroom battles with Shirley Howe Manson. This had been the first such case that Wardell had ever lost, thoroughly and finally.

Morton Zannis, a private detective, had been involved in several prominent divorce cases himself; had been accused of wiretapping and perjury in the trial of the boiler room operators Corsi and O'Donnell and had served a six-months term for contempt of court following their conviction. Also he had been held as a material witness in the murder of the gambler Manny Goldstein and had kept the newspapers informed of the progress of the investigation into this case, thus arousing the anger of the district attorney and the police.

Louis Balthazar's name had been cropping up for years in newspapers in connection with a wide variety of antisocial activities, and he had served two short terms on Riker's Island, one for gambling and the second for vagrancy. However, he had suddenly gone "respectable" some five years ago and had been taken up by New York's cafe society as a much sought-after guest and a welcome host. His front was selling insurance, and he seemed to have unlimited funds for entertainment. He was supposed to own several oil wells, and he was a constant escort for aspiring debs on the fringes of notoriety and for moving picture actresses who visited New York. He had been listed as the producer for one year of Dr. Finstone's television program, "Charity Begins at Home."

Zannis and Balthazar had been arrested in an early morning raid on a suite of offices in the Lackey Building on Fifth Avenue, in which had been found the most elaborate and modern electronic devices for tapping telephones and recording telephone conversations that the police ever had encountered. In the words of Deputy Inspector Charles O'Hare, who led the raid, "This is the finest equipment of its kind I've ever seen. Most of it I never even knew existed. The installation obviously was made by an expert—I'd even call him a genius."

The taps were on the private telephones of a score or so New Yorkers who collectively had more influence on the fluctuations of Wall Street prices than any group in the country. Among them were Winfield Stokes of the private banking firm of Finchley, Stokes, Limited; George Downes of United Electric; Hanna Prentice and Winchell Manson, both of whom were lost on the Oceanic airliner; Willis Harrington of Oceanic; Colonel Wilson Gaylord, publisher of the *Press* and chairman of the board of Eastern Paper Mills; the Goldstone Brothers, Morris and Herschel, who owned railroads, bus and trucking lines; and Morrow Simpson of International Radio and Television. These were the only names run in the *Press* story, but there were many more just as prominent and powerful whose phones had been tapped.

An hour after the arrest of Zannis and Balthazar, Luke Wardell was seized in his home on East 73rd Street, Manhattan, and taken to police headquarters by Inspector

O'Hare and two detectives. He was questioned there briefly by O'Hare and Deputy Commissioner Gordon Buell, then arraigned with Balthazar and Zannis before a magistrate. The three were held in bail of $5,000 each, pending action by the grand jury, but within an hour Wardell supplied the bail for all three and they were released.

But December 13 was the day that the FBI released to the press services the announcement that the airliner, which carried Greta Fortune and the forty-seven others to their deaths, had been sabotaged. The headlines in the *Press* read:

OCEANIC PLANE, LOST WITH 48, WAS TIME-BOMBED, SAYS FBI

So the story of the wiretapping and extortion was not developed as fully as it could have been, or should have been. There was too much competition.

Wardell, Zannis and Balthazar were indicted the following Monday by the grand jury, were rearrested shortly thereafter, then released again in bail of $5,000 each, once again supplied by Wardell. The story in the *Press* was adequate, giving a more complete picture of the wiretapping operation that District Attorney Michael Grady charged had been installed for the purpose of ferreting out industrial and financial secrets and using the information for stock market manipulation. Once again the story was on an inside page; there just wasn't any room on page one with the sensational developments of the Oceanic airliner sabotage.

This estimate of the story's value was not concurred with, however, by Lawrence Keene, financial editor of the *Press*. He was tremendously excited by the wiretapping revelations, and he spoke to both Finley Browne and Judd Victory about them.

"This story is going to shake Wall Street right down to its sewer," he told Browne. "Let me give you some background on it—a series of six or seven articles."

Browne shook his head. "We haven't got an inch of space, Larry. We're running eight or ten columns under what we should have for this airplane story. Write it, sure, but run it back in your own pages. You've got more room back there than we have for all the news of the world."

"You're making a mistake," said Larry. "It's worth page one, plane or no plane. There isn't a guy in all lower Manhattan who hasn't been affected by this."

Browne was adamant, so Larry Keene went next to Judd Victory and made his pitch. He caught Victory at a bad time—the second afternoon edition coming up and a makeup editor who had had one too many martinis at lunch.

"Not today," he exclaimed. "Christ, who gives a damn about those thieves down in Wall Street."

Keene then went to Colonel Gaylord's office—after all, his private phone had been tapped along with all the rest—and sat patiently and waited for nearly an hour before the publisher would see him. The man who came out of the publisher's office was Michael Grady, district attorney of New York County.

"Hello, Mike."

"Hello, Larry. What's new?"

"Not much, Mike. One thing I wanted to ask you, though. Who was Wardell working for?"

"Wardell? For himself."

Larry shook his head. "No, Mike. You know better than that."

The district attorney looked at the financial editor and smiled. They were a couple of Fordham boys and had known each other since P.S. 153 and the area around 103rd Street and Amsterdam Avenue in the twenties. In those days Mike

Grady had always been the leader and Larry Keene the follower—sometimes a first lieutenant but never the originator or the planner.

"Do you know?" asked Grady.

"I'll be seeing you," said Larry Keene, turning and opening the door of the publisher's office.

Publisher and financial editor greeted each other warmly. Wilson Gaylord had great respect for Larry Keene and considered him the best financial editor in the country and one of its best reporters. Larry liked his publisher because he gave him a free hand in reporting the machinations of Wall Street and never attempted to censor his copy, even when Gaylord's own interests were involved. It may have been the best way to handle Larry Keene at that. Seldom had he ever written anything that would harm the publisher, even though Larry had found Gaylord connected with transactions of which he disapproved.

"You having trouble with Grady?" Larry asked him.

Colonel Gaylord laughed. "He wants to be *Governor* Larry. And a handsome governor he would make. Maybe we need another virile Irishman up in Albany."

"Mike's too slick for me," said Larry. "I don't go for the type, though I've always liked him personally."

"I presume you came to see me about Wardell and company," said Gaylord, fixing Larry Keene with his grey eyes.

Larry nodded. "I'd like to do a series on this, Colonel Gaylord. You know what's behind it, probably better than I do. I think we should give it a good play, out on page one."

"What does Judd Victory say?"

"In a word—no. He's got no time for it, with the airplane story running."

"I would say he's right, Larry. There's nothing as big that, and there hasn't been for years... What's your angle on Wardell?"

"There's a real stink behind this, colonel. It would depend upon whom Wardell was working for, and I've got a strong hunch about that. I'll have it verified soon enough."

"Who?"

"Well, look at it this way. The person who could get information from the private telephones of the top financial manipulators of the country could just about write his own ticket. He could gain control of any companies; he could wreck financial empires; he could amass billions, given enough time. The harm he could do is impossible to calculate and the fortunes he could seize are limitless."

"That doesn't fit anyone I know," said Gaylord.

"It does if you consider one thing—he hasn't been operating this racket very long so he hasn't gone very far with it. Who, would you say, is the top fast-buck boy of the country today? Who has made all of the recent phenomenal killings on Wall Street, and has seized control of a half a dozen big companies in the past year?"

Gaylord opened his eyes wide and slammed a hand on his desk. "Lamar Hinemann!" he exclaimed.

"Sure. Lamar Hinemann. And his body's floating around right now in the middle of the Atlantic."

Pete Morehouse had a staff of three girls who clipped all editions of the eight New York newspapers, plus a score or so of Long Island, Westchester, and New Jersey dailies. Another girl, a boy, and Pete himself did the sorting and filing, but Pete managed to glance over everything that was filed each day, though he seldom read a story through. His thirty-odd years of practice reading newspapers enabled him to get the gist of a story in seconds. One story in a thousand would he find a name or an incident that would click in his prodigious memory, and these stories he would pause over to digest every detail, sometimes putting them aside in the top drawer of his desk for further perusal. It was not that Pete ever used this collection of information and names any more. As head of the library of the *Press*, he wasn't required to know anything more about anybody in the world except where to find the information about him if it was required. But his lifetime as a reporter and assistant city editor had so strongly formed his habits and his routines of thinking that it was quite impossible for him to do other than he did. And besides all of that, he enjoyed it. It gave him something to do that was familiar.

The story from the *Atlantic City Courier* was nothing of interest. A list of real estate transactions. Pete was about to throw the clipping into the discard pile when a name down in the middle of the story leaped out at him, Mrs. Mildred Gower. He read the paragraph about her:

The Elite Restaurant on the Boardwalk has been purchased by Mrs. Mildred Gower of Brooklyn, N.Y. The deal was consummated through Smith & Hyde, brokers, representing the seller, the Bascom estate, and the reported price paid by Mrs. Gower is $82,000. Mr. Hyde said Mrs. Gower paid the entire amount in cash and will take possession of the premises within two weeks.

Pete sent for the clippings on Willard Gower and extracted from its envelope the *Times* story he had read the week before. He was right. The name of the wife of the man who had died under the subway train at Chambers Street with a $1,000 bill in his pocket, was Mildred.

She had told the *Times* reporter that she could not account for the fact of her husband's having that much money. Yet ten days after his death she was paying $82,000 for a restaurant in Atlantic City.

Fran Addams came into Pete's office carrying coffee in a container and a sandwich, and he showed her the clippings. She read them through while she munched on her sandwich, then handed them back to Pete.

"That ought to make Yerbe happy," she said. "He's been boring everyone to death about the man he saw mangled under the subway train."

"Is Yerbe working today, Fran?"

"No. I think it's his day off. I haven't seen him around."

Pete picked up the phone and told the operator, "See if you can get me Carl Yerbe at his home. If he's not in, leave word for him to call me."

Within a minute the phone rang back. It was Yerbe.

"I've got something that might interest you," said Pete. "This Willard Gower. His wife's name is Mildred. She's just bought a restaurant at Atlantic City for $82,000."

"What do you know?" exclaimed Yerbe. "Maybe there's a story there after all, eh?"

"Maybe," said Pete. "You got time to drop around and see her?"

"See her? What for?"

"For the story," said Pete patiently. He was used to young reporters who didn't know what to do next. "You want to learn to be a newspaper man, don't you? Well, this is how you do it. You go interview Willard Gower's widow."

"Sure. I'll do that... What do I ask her?"

"The first question," said Pete, "is where she got the $82,000."

"Sure, but—what difference would that make?"

"It may make a difference if she tells you the truth," said Pete. "That's a lot of money for the widow of a man like Gower to put her hands on."

"O.K.," said Yerbe doubtfully. "I'll try."

"She'll probably resent your question. You've got to be very diplomatic. You've got to get her confidence—get her to like you so she'll talk."

"O.K. Then what?"

"Phone me and tell me what you've found out. If I've left, call me at home. You can get me through the switchboard."

"Will do," said Yerbe. "What's her address?"

Pete gave him the Sterling Place number. When he had hung up, Fran Addams asked, "What have you got cooking on that back burner of yours, Pete?"

He shrugged. "Just a hunch, Fran. It'll probably turn out to be a bust. These hunches of mine always do. But somehow I've just got to find out what happens *after* the story—what becomes of the people who were in yesterday's newspaper. This Gower, now. He was killed under a subway train, and there was a thousand-dollar bill in his pocket. His wife said she had never seen a thousand-dollar bill. She said, 'We are not wealthy people,' implying that they were not the kind of people who would have such a bill or such a sum of money. So now she pays out $82,000 in cash for a restaurant at Atlantic City. It doesn't add up."

"What's your hunch, then?"

"That this guy Gower was murdered, for one thing. Those two men whom the motorman saw with him—I think they pushed him off the platform in front of the train."

"That doesn't leave you anywhere," said Fran.

"But everything would be explained if you knew why he was murdered."

"*If* he was murdered. You don't expect to find that out talking to Mrs. Gower, do you?"

"No. But suppose she won't tell where she got the money? That'll indicate something very peculiar about all this. And I'm betting that she won't say a word."

"It sounds as though it has possibilities the way you tell it," said Fran. "You want another reporter to work on your story?"

"Sure," said Pete. "You got time?"

"I'll make time. What can I do?"

"Well, if you could go around to that radio shop on Nassau Street"—he picked up the clipping and read off the address—"it's at 116½. The guy's name is Erhardt. He was Gower's partner. See what you can find out. Anything. Who Gower's friends were, what jobs he was doing—things like that."

"You think he's going to tell me anything interesting?" asked Fran.

"No, I don't. I think he'll tell you a lot of lies if he talks to you at all. That he'll cover up all the way around. But we can match anything he says with what Mrs. Gower will tell Yerbe, and maybe we can pick out something... If you could see him today while Yerbe is interviewing her, it would be a lot better."

"I'll try to get Mr. Browne to let me off early. I'll develop some sudden female complaint."

"Fine...Fran, you know this is probably all a waste of time?"

"Maybe not," she replied. "How can you tell so early?"

CHAPTER SIX

LARRY KEENE called on Luke Wardell at 7:30 P.M., on December 16 at Wardell's home on East 73rd Street, one of a score of private dwellings in the block between Lexington and Third that had successfully resisted the encroachment of apartment buildings. It was a renovated and modernized brownstone, with the entrance on the street floor instead of up a flight, as the house had been originally planned. Larry rang the bell, waited about a minute, then was admitted by a stony-faced butler with the round head of the eastern Mediterranean.

"I am Lawrence Keene of the *Press*," he said. "I phoned Mr. Wardell's secretary this afternoon and told her I would call."

"Mr. Wardell will see you," said the butler. He had only a slight accent. "You will give me your hat and coat?"

Larry handed them to him, then followed him up the stairway and to a huge room furnished as a library on the second floor in the rear. Luke Wardell greeted him at the door and put an arm around his shoulder as he led him into the room.

"What would you like to drink, Larry?"

"Scotch, if it's available."

"Everything's available in this menage—everything but wiretaps, that is."

"It's some different from that apartment on West 54th Street," said Larry as Wardell mixed the drink at a small portable bar. "Gone are the red plush chairs, the oriental, rugs and the occidental blondes..."

Luke handed Larry his drink and the latter sat on a divan facing a Georgian fireplace encased in bookshelves. Wardell took a deep leather chair to his left and picked up his own highball from the coffee table.

"Here's to Mike Grady," Wardell said, "valedictorian of the class of thirty-four."

Larry raised his glass. "Here's to Luke Wardell, who was too smart to be valedictorian."

Wardell laughed. "Maybe you've got something there."

"It's not that I give anything to Mike Grady," said Larry. "I don't have a very high opinion of politicians. None of them."

"And criminal attorneys who get themselves indicted?"

"About the same. But hell, Luke, I didn't come here to judge you. I came for information. I imagine you've got it all figured how to beat this rap, or you never would have let yourself into it."

"That's right, Larry. So we'll start at the beginning. Who do you suppose tipped off the cops about the wiretap setup in the first place?"

"I wouldn't know. Don't tell me it was Luke Wardell himself?"

"Give the man sixty-four silver dollars. I'll tell you what it's about, Larry, but I've got to ask you one thing. I've got to ask you that you don't print any of it—not yet."

"And nuts to you, Luke. I'll print what I damn please. If you don't tell me, I'll find out elsewhere. You know that."

"You'll find out some of it, maybe."

"Let's start out with what I know already and what I'm going to print tomorrow," said Larry Keene. "Let me tell you first so that there'll be no misunderstanding. The way I figure it, you have been the front man for this wiretap operation. You didn't have the wiretaps installed, and you've had nothing to do with any of the information recorded from the various telephones. In fact, you've heard only a very few of the tapes, if any. Is that correct?"

"Yes," said Luke, "that's substantially correct."

"Now the man you're working for in this…that's the big ace in the hole. That's the big secret. That's what you suppose no one in the world knows. Correct?"

"Yes. Nobody does know."

"How about Lamar Hinemann. Does that name ring any bells?"

"Yes, I know Lamar Hinemann."

"In fact, you receive a yearly retainer from him, don't you?"

"Where'd you find that out, Larry?"

"Income tax, I do favors for them and they do favors for me."

"I can't deny that I receive a retainer from Hinemann—"

"Fine. Lamar Hinemann is the owner of the Lackey Building wiretap. Lamar Hinemann is the man who received all of the tapes from the recorders. Correct or not?"

"I can't answer that."

"You mean you won't answer that. Well, never you mind. Buy tomorrow's *Press* and you'll read all about it. It won't be on page one. Back in my column. But it'll all be there."

"I wouldn't if I were you," said Wardell. "I'm talking to you as my friend now, Larry. Not as an attorney and certainly not as the pigeon who got himself indicted. Leave Hinemann's name out of it or there'll be the Goddamndest explosion since the little black wagon stopped in front of the stock exchange. That I can promise you."

"Fine," said Keene. "If that's what will happen, then that's exactly what we need in this rotten mess. Maybe an explosion will blow some of it away, eh?"

"That's not the point," said Wardell. "If Hinemann got the information and used it for his own ends, well and good—or bad, as the case may be. I don't care about Hinemann personally, not one iota. But there are a lot of innocent people associated with him who will be absolutely ruined."

"Luke Wardell rides again. Now you're worried about innocent people?"

"Sure. The governors of two states, for instance. How about that?"

"Politicians."

"One cabinet officer. One of the most respected men in Washington."

"He was just another sucker to Hinemann, and he deserves nothing more than any other sucker ever got. Don't waste your breath, Luke. I wouldn't layoff this story for my own mother. God rest her. And she'd have too much integrity to ask me to."

"You mean that?"

"Yep."

"O.K. I'll verify Hinemann for you, if that's what you want."

"It's exactly what I want. What else would drive me out into the cold on a night like this?"

"It was Hinemann's wiretap. If you're going to print that tomorrow, I'll just have to revise my plans. No great harm done. But I've got one favor to ask in return for this verification."

"I'm in a trading mood. Shoot."

"Leave Judy Hinemann out of it. She knows nothing about the taps or about any of her late husband's business. Absolutely nothing."

"That means she does, eh?"

"No! For God's sake, Larry. Stop being a newspaperman for a moment and act like a human being. The point of all of this is Judy. She's the reason I turned the whole thing in to the police—so we could get rid of it forever."

"And then?"

Luke Wardell shrugged and got up. He went to the bar and mixed two more drinks. He carried them back to the coffee table, putting one in front of Larry Keene, and sat down.

"You going to knock off this luscious Judy?" Larry asked as he sipped his drink.

"That's a crude way of putting it, friend."

"Well—you going to marry her and the Hinemann millions."

"Could be."

"You're not the marrying type, Luke. In fact you're the most dedicated misogynist I know."

"I *was,* Larry; make that past tense."

"All right. For true love, I'll do it. Nothing about Judy. Couldn't you have just shut up the wiretap and gone home, without all of this grandstand play?"

"Impossible."

"Why not?"

"It was too good a thing. There were other people involved, and they wouldn't have had it that way."

"People like Judy Hinemann?"

"All right, damn it, people like Judy Hinemann. But now it's out of her hands, and it's out of everyone's hands. So we start all over. And in six months or so Judy and I will be married. That's the way it is."

Larry sat in silence, sipping his Scotch. It was difficult to admit to himself that he didn't like Luke Wardell any more. He and Luke had been inseparable friends during his last two years at Fordham. They had once thought alike about everything—girls, politics, religion, what was acceptable in the behavior of men and women, how the world should be run. Twenty years ago it had all seemed rather simple. One had ethics, one had honor, one would never compromise with evil.

"You were going to tell me about the wiretap," said Larry.

"No reason why not. It'll all come out at the trial. The original wiretap was set up by Morton Zannis in the Lackey Building for the Winchell Manson divorce case of a couple of years ago. You remember that, don't you?"

"Sure. Shirley Howe Manson. Is that how she got the information about her various rivals?"

"That's how. You may or may not remember that I defended Manson in that case. Nobody could figure out where Shirley was getting her information. Then right in the middle of the trial she got Louis Balthazar and some of his hoodlum friends to raid Manson's hideout up on Park Avenue, and she nailed him to the cross. There wasn't anything I could do after that. She got her divorce and a couple of million dollars. Shirley was a smart little girl."

"In one sense, yes. Then what happened?"

"Manson and I were beaten, but I couldn't let it go at that. I knew Balthazar, and I got hold of him and persuaded him to talk. He told me about the wiretap. One thing led to another, and I got him to take me to the Lackey Building and show it to me. I met Zannis up there—for the first time, I may say—and I found that the tap was still operating, that Zannis had it hooked up to a half a dozen phones and had installed a tape recorder.

"I had quite a talk with Zannis and Balthazar. We discussed the legal—or illegal—aspects of wiretapping, and I told them where they stood with the law. I'll admit, Larry, that their setup gave me ideas and that I wasn't beyond considering its use for my own ends, if a case should come my way where information of that sort could be useful. But I made no deal with them, beyond promising to represent them in the event of their arrest. I did not know specifically what they intended to use the wiretaps for, nor was aware at that time that this service they were setting up was going to be for sale as such. I knew nothing about business and financial espionage, nor would I have condoned it.

"The matter rested there for a year. Then in November of 1956 I got a call from Lamar Hinemann's office. I went down to the Eastern Building and met a man there who shall remain nameless, and was retained as attorney on a yearly basis for a company called Fifth Avenue Recording. I admit that the retainer was substantial and that I was pleased with the client. The business of Fifth Avenue Recording was and is, to my knowledge, legitimate. I know nothing about electronics, and so I did not inquire too deeply, beyond the knowledge that I would be associated with Morton Zannis and Louis Balthazar, among others.

"There it is, Larry. I admit the association but I deny participation. The indictment means nothing. Mike Grady is just hysterical over this and is hitting out in all directions."

"Is that all?" asked Larry Keene.

"Yes. That's the whole story."

Larry shook his head. "It's a very small part of the story," he said. "It's such a small part that it's practically nothing."

"That's all I know," protested Wardell. "I can't tell you what I don't know about."

"Where do the two governors and the cabinet member come in?"

"Ah—that has nothing to do with this, only indirectly. Naturally I have learned a great deal about the secondary aspects of this operation—what the information was used for and by whom it was used. But I don't intend to go into that, and I am certain that Mike Grady won't. Mike has more sense than that."

"Maybe he has," said Larry, "but I haven't. You see, Luke, I'm not planning to run for governor."

Wardell shook his head. "Your libel lawyer down on the *Press* won't let you run any of those names," he said. "Sure you're O.K. with Hinemann, he's dead. But if you mention anyone else, you'll be sued from hell to breakfast."

"So it was a group operation, then, and Hinemann was just the front man?"

"The front man *and* the brains," replied the attorney. "I was Hinemann's idea, so far as I know, but he didn't have the capital to swing it on an effective scale."

"This was a year ago, eh? I thought Hinemann had plenty then—something over fifty million."

"No, Hinemann was just about broke a year ago. Not many knew it; in fact I found it out only a few weeks ago. He'd got himself caught in that Arabian oil deal you may remember, and then on top of that he just missed getting control of Pennsylvania Central, and when that stock dived he lost every cent of his reserve... A year ago, Larry, he would have shot himself if he could have afforded to buy a box of bullets."

"I'm damned," exclaimed Keene. "Well, how's he done this past year?"

"His estate will assay over one hundred million," said Wardell. "That's what I'm talking about—there's too much involved in this wiretap for you or anyone to start riding white horses. Sure, talk about Hinemann, if you want, but leave the rest of them out of it."

"Including Judy Starr, eh?"

"She was fronting for some people, too," said Wardell morosely. "That's one thing that worries me about her Larry. I don't like her friends."

"You want to tell me who they are?"

Wardell shook his head. "No."

"What's your defense going to be, Luke?"

"At the eavesdropping trial? Simply that I represent Zannis and Balthazar and Hinemann as attorney and that I was never informed of the wiretapping nor in any other way was aware of its existence."

"How'd you get arrested then, and indicted?"

"That puzzles me," said Luke. "There is nothing so far as I know to connect me with this operation except my name as an officer of Fifth Avenue Recording. Well, I'll find out soon enough, I suppose."

Larry Keene got up to leave, explaining he was to meet his wife for dinner. Wardell followed him downstairs and helped him with his coat. At the door Larry turned and asked one more question.

"I promised I'd ask this for a friend," he said. "Guy down on the paper named Pete Morehouse, who seems to be interested in this for reasons of his own. What Pete wants to know is, who was the electronic genius who installed the wiretaps and the tape recorders?"

"Is this strictly off the record?" asked Wardell.

"Sure enough. It's not for me. Pete's in charge of the library, and he couldn't use it if he would."

"O.K. Little man by the name of Gower. I don't remember his first name. He certainly knows his business."

"He did know it," said Larry. "Not any more."

Cissie Morehouse was annoyed. The telephone had rung a dozen times within the last half hour, and Pete had been talking on it almost constantly, leaving her sitting with the best pinochle hand she'd ever held, good for at least 500 if she drew anything at all. Finally Pete came into the living room from the kitchen, where the downstairs phone was located.

"That was Carl Yerbe," he said. "That kid might make a reporter one of these days."

"Well, are we going to talk about Yerbe, or are we going to finish this hand?"

Pete resumed his chair at the card table and picked up his cards. "O.K. Let's play. The story can wait."

"What story?"

"The one I've been working on. This little guy Gower, who was killed at the Chambers street subway station."

"What about him?"

"You want to play pinochle or you want me to talk?"

"Well…we can play cards any time. What about Gower?"

"It's his wife. You remember I told you they found a one-thousand-dollar bill in his pocket? Well, his wife told a reporter from the *Times* that she'd never seen that much money—that she couldn't account for it. She told a story about her husband phoning her and saying he was going to meet somebody to collect some money. So today I ran across an item in the *Atlantic City Courier* that said she had bought an $82,000 restaurant on the Boardwalk. I sent Yerbe out to see her, and you know what she told him? She said she was buying the restaurant for someone else, she wouldn't say who."

"Whom."

"O.K. Whom. She said she was going to run it with the other person, but she refused to give him any more information."

"Well?"

"A likely story. People don't give other people $82,00 just like that to go out and buy a restaurant for them."

"No, not to strangers. But suppose it was some member of her own family. Suppose, say, it was her brother."

"Yeah, I can see that. I didn't think of that... So now we got to find out who her brother is."

"That's right," said Cissie. "Or maybe her father or uncle."

"You know, Cissie, you've got something there. Let's say she's telling the truth."

"What else did she tell Yerbe?"

"That's all. She wouldn't say why Atlantic City had been selected or who selected it. She wouldn't tell him anything. She seemed scared when he walked in, he said, and she just clammed up on him. So I guess that's that."

"Who else called you—that call just before Yerbe?"

"That was Fran Addams. She'd been over to see this Gower's partner, Kurt Erhardt. She found out absolute nothing. Erhardt gave her the bum's rush out of the shop as soon as she told him who she was. She said he's a big, tough character and he really scared her. So we haven't got anything more than we had this morning."

"Sure you have," said Cissie. "You've got a good lead on that $82,000, haven't you?"

Pete thought and scratched his head. "I see what you mean. The tax angle, eh? She's got to account for that, sooner or later. Why not sooner? I show up with the Atlantic City clipping and I say, 'Madam, I'm from the Bureau of Internal Revenue. How about this item of $82,000 for this restaurant? You going to declare that in your income tax this year? Boy, will *that* floor her."

"That's a mean thing even to think of, Pete Morehouse!"

"Well, it's one way to do it. You know what I think?"

"What, honey?"

"I think that after I break this story, I'm going to be back on the street again, where I belong. A reporter."

"Well I hope so," said Cissie. "I'm certainly getting sick of your eternal griping."

Just as they started to play out their pinochle hand the telephone rang again. Pete went to answer it and heard Larry Keene's voice on the other end.

"Hi, Larry."

"Pete, I found out something for you. The guy who installed the equipment in that Lackey Building wiretap setup was named Gower."

"Well, well…"

"He's the guy that was killed at Chambers Street, with the thousand-dollar bill in his pocket."

"Yeah, I know. Willard Gower."

"It looks like it might develop into a story."

"That's what I think," said Pete. "I'm working on some other stuff to go with it."

"O.K. Be seeing you."

CHAPTER SEVEN

ON TUESDAY MORNING, December 17, Calvin Colby, Special Agent In Charge of the New York office, FBI, called on Willis Harrington, president of Oceanic Airlines. Colby didn't actively resent the necessity for making this call, but he did consider it a waste of time, and he was conscience that it was contrary to the usual routine of the Bureau. He was well aware by this time that Mr. Harrington and the attorney general were close friends and that the Department of Justice was especially concerned with the views and opinions of Oceanic Airlines. However, Colby did have to admit, in all fairness that Willis Harrington had not in any way put on any pressure and that he had made no demands nor in any unethical way traded upon his friendship with the attorney general. He had merely expressed a desire to know in depth the progress of the investigation into the sabotage of Flight 900 of December 5. As for the rest of it, Colby had been told exactly what to do by the director of the Bureau.

The FBI man took a chair in front of Harrington's desk and opened his briefcase on his knees. "I don't know just how much of this you want to see," he said. "I've brought most of the file. There are several reports as yet unfinished and I did not bring those."

"I'll tell you one thing that I am interested in," said Harrington, leaning forward and speaking in a low, confidential voice. "We've got a big organization, too big for us to keep track of in any detailed way. I know all of our key personnel, of course. I know them personally and well, and I know most of their foibles and weaknesses, and think I can vouch for them, one by one. But there are hundreds that I don't know anything about. When something like this happens, I worry about that."

"I see," said Colby, arranging his papers on the desk. "Then you are interested mainly in the employees of Oceanic Airways?"

"Yes. Of course, if you've found out anything else that points to a solution of this mass murder, then I would want to know about that, too."

"We haven't. I can tell you that very frankly. We've dug up a mountain of information about a great number of people, and much of it is tremendously interesting and of potential value. But there hasn't been a break yet. There is no conclusive evidence pointing to any one person or group of persons that would enable us to concentrate our efforts and work out a solution."

"That's not very hopeful," said Harrington, leaning back in his chair.

"Considering the little time we have spent on the investigation, I can't say that I agree with you, Mr. Harrington. I understand your impatience and your urgency, but it is not reasonable to expect that we are going to crack this case in the first few days."

"It didn't take the FBI very long to light on the Graham boy in that Denver plane sabotage."

"Yes, that case had unusual aspects right from the start. Some three days after our investigation had begun we were led to concentrate our efforts on Graham, and three days after that we had his confession. It was not until he confessed that we were able to collect all of the evidence we needed to make a case against him. That, of course, is just the opposite of the expected procedure. Usually we collect the evidence first, then confront our suspect and get his confession. In the loss of your airliner, Mr. Harrington, I may say that right now we are overwhelmed by the wealth of information, on the one hand, and defeated by the lack of any specific and conclusive clues, on the other. But this is a situation to be expected at this stage. The vital facts we need will clarify themselves, and then we shall know where to go."

"Your confidence gives me optimism. Will you tell me, now, about our own people, Mr. Colby?"

The FBI agent picked up a file and opened it. "I'll begin with William Kerr Lovejoy, your chief of maintenance. We have investigated all of those who had opportunity—who had access to the airliner before it took off on its fatal flight. Lovejoy was one of the last to inspect this plane, and he was inside the forward baggage compartment just before the plane was towed to the loading ramp. Let me read you parts of this report. It is not particularly significant, but it will demonstrate to you the thoroughness with which we are pursuing this inquiry.

"*Lovejoy was born in Greenoch, Scotland, on the Clyde, on January 3, 1902. His father was Charles Lovejoy, a machinist, and his mother Clara Kerr Lovejoy, housewife. At the age of five he was brought to America by his parents, who settled in New York City on the upper West Side. He attended public schools in New York and graduated from Evander Childs High School in 1920 with average grades. During the last three years of high school he worked part time (summers full time) as an apprentice machinist at the Fuller-McCulloch Machine Shop, where his father was foreman.*

"*The Lovejoys were a quarrelsome family and young William's earliest recollection of his parents was with their voices raised in dispute. Up until the age of ten he had a sister Irma, a year older than himself, who added her shrewish temper to the family bickering. Irma died at the age of eleven from lumbar pneumonia. At the age of eighteen one week after his graduation from Evander Childs, William left home, never to return. He saw his father just once up to his death in 1949, encountering him in a Times Square bar on a Saturday night. He saw his mother never.*

"William went west, hitch-hiking, riding freight trains and, on occasion, walking. In August 1920 he arrived in San Diego in fairly good condition, and he got a job with Duke McKay's Air Circus as mechanic at ten dollars a week. He discovered his love for airplanes and everything about them, but particularly their engines. They were the first objects he ever did love.

"As for love, it was a word that has little personal meaning for William Lovejoy. He had heard the word occasionally in his home; his mother had said that she loved him and his father likewise, and he had told both of his parents that he loved them. But he didn't know what he meant when he said it, since the word was accompanied by no feeling of which he was aware. It was merely a formula that he used, like 'How are you?' when he met someone he knew, not in the least caring how he was.

"Girls had never interested him enough for him to make advances to them or seek their company. When he thought of girls, he thought of his shrewish sister, who had died, or he thought of his mother with her tired, accusing voice and her grim mouth. Females were not objects of love because of their femaleness. Even after puberty he did not yearn for them to 'love' them. Maybe for sexual satisfaction, but he had never been bothered enough by his sexual urges to force him into the company of girls.

"On the night of July 4, 1921, when he was nineteen years old William Lovejoy went out on a double date with a Henry Matson, parachute jumper with the circus, in Butte, Montana. Matson, twenty-two, had picked up two town girls, who had come sightseeing to the field that had been rented for the planes and equipment. Matson had found the girls inseparable. He had insisted that William take one, a blonde by the name of Eve, with no remembered marks of distinction. The four of them got into Duke McKay's car, an old Essex McKay had taken in trade for a washed-out airplane, and they went riding into the woods. It was a balmy evening. They drove off the road among the pines to a clearing the girls knew. Matson and his girl got out of the car to go for a walk.

"William sat in the back seat with Eve. He didn't know what to do, so he did nothing. Presently Eve asked him if he didn't want to kiss her. He did, with his lips tight shut and she laughed at him. She told him she would show him how to kiss. She told him to open his mouth, and then she pressed her lips to his and put her tongue in his mouth. She told him that that was what he was supposed to do. He did it but he didn't like it. It seemed nasty to him—and he didn't like her breath. Very reluctantly he followed her lead and attempted to accede to her demands, but he succeeded only in making her angry.

"William didn't know why she should be angry. He told her to go to hell, and he got out of the car and walked around. A week later he discovered he had contracted a venereal disease. It was long lasting and extremely painful, and he never forgot it. So Eve was not only the first girl he ever loved—she was the last.

"One can understand Lovejoy's misogynism on the basis of this experience and earlier indications of a lack of sexual drive. The rest of his hates are too obscure to be easily analyzed. Whether or not these hates have any significance in this overall problem is difficult to judge. Lovejoy hates the notion of a home and family life; he hates the acquisition of belongings of any sort beyond the bare necessities and he hates all of the general classes of civilized society, especially the rich and the very poor; he detests all politicians, political activities and the various political parties; hates the members of various professions, particularly lawyers, bankers and other financiers; he has contempt for communists and capitalists alike, and he confesses candidly that insofar as the passengers themselves were concerned the destruction of the Triton airliner was no loss to the world. His only regret centers on the airplane itself. The loss appears to be a grievous one to him.

"Here are some facts that are missing: Lovejoy says he knows nothing about explosives but this has not been verified. He denies that he carried anything on board the lost Triton and there is no record that he did. But also there is no proof that he did not. There is nothing at this stage of the inquiry that connects Lovejoy with any of the passengers on Flight 900."

Colby stopped reading and looked up at Harrington. "Your chief of maintenance is hardly a suspect on the basis of this," he said.

"No, I would say not. How about the rest of the maintenance people?"

"We've gone into them thoroughly. We've found nothing. I think you will agree with me that the maintenance department is an unlikely area to find the sort of person we are hunting for. However, we have taken nothing for granted."

"How about the plane crew?" asked Harrington. "We know little about them—too little, I think."

"I will read you one report," said Colby. "It is the only one with any possibilities, but you will agree, I am sure, the possibilities are limited. This is the report concerning Fred Lochman, the pilot of Flight 900, and his widow, Marjorie Cassell Lochman. You will note that she has the same name as Mark Cassell, the husband of Greta Fortune. We have found that they were first cousins, a fact that seems to have no significance.

"I presume you know much about Lochman, who was one of your senior pilots, his war record and such facts. This is what our agents report:

"Lochman was normally cantankerous and bad-tempered with his friends but pleasant enough to strangers. He had been married three times. The first Mrs. Lochman was a schoolmate from McKeesport High School, who bore him a son and got a divorce shortly afterwards on grounds of desertion. The second was a girl with society aspirations who didn't achieve them, despite her banker-father's money, and who divorced Lochman in Reno for no apparent reason. She continued to live with him after the divorce and up to the time of his third marriage.

"The third Mrs. Lochman is a girl named Marjorie Cassell, who had been a stewardess on the Oceanic's Trans-Atlantic run, but had never flown in Lochman's crew. She is a small, vivacious brunette of

twenty-eight (she claims twenty-three), with blue eyes that have a wide, innocent look, and a figure that attracts much attention.

"Lochman, forty-three, is described as handsome, athletic and willful. He arrived at Oceanic Operations at 2:30 P.M., December 5, carrying a small overnight bag, which he checked with flight baggage. The bag was unusually heavy, and he told the baggage clerk to handle it carefully because there was a bottle of brandy in it, a present from his wife, to keep up his spirits during the long Atlantic night. He then picked up his passport (which was kept at Operations), bought $100 worth of francs at the current New York rate, then went to the pilots' room and met the members of his crew. He introduced himself to those he did not know; he had flown with several of them before. He told the senior stewardess that he was glad she was with him again, and he told the junior stewardess that she had pretty eyes. This last remark was accompanied by a pat on her backside, which apparently is considered to be a not unusual airline pleasantry.

"Lochman spoke to his crew for about fifteen minutes, telling them what he expected of them individually and as a group, making it clear where he wanted each stationed in the event of an emergency. He rubbed his hand over his brow several times during this talk, and others in the pilots' room who knew him got the impression that he had a hangover and was finding it difficult going.

"After this briefing, Lochman went through the usual routine of flight planning, weather study, working out the minimum time route to Paris-Orly (FFOL), figuring fuel consumption and total fuel weight necessary, selecting an alternate field in the event Orly should shut down (Geneva-HEGE), and then making out the flight plan in duplicate, the copy for air traffic control. This flight plan was for all land areas only. The navigator was making out his own plan for the over-waters areas, from GAR to 20 West, and filling his own duplicate with A.T.C.

"John Casper, the co-pilot, who was a bright, eager youth of twenty-six, had made out another flight plan meanwhile, and he offered it to Lochman. The captain glanced at it briefly, then wadded it up and threw it in a nearby wastebasket. He told Casper in the hearing of *others, 'I'll do the planning. You've got plenty of duties to keep you busy.'*

"Lochman's final order in operations was for 1,000 pounds more of fuel, which would bring the Triton up to 150,000 pounds take-off weight. Then he cleared the flight with the dispatcher and called his navigator, Donald Walters, and the two left operations together for the U.S. Weather Bureau for the official weather briefing, a federal government requirement for all flights. Lochman and Walters together listened to the ten-minute analysis by forecaster James Davis, picked up copies of the North-Atlantic weather charts for that period, and departed. Neither spoke to Davis beyond the bare amenities.

"Lochman boarded the Triton at 7:36, accompanied by the navigator. He was seen to take his place in the left-hand seat of the cockpit. At 7:51, he signaled the ground crew that he would start the inboard port engine. At intervals of thirty seconds or so, he started the other three engines, then taxied the plane slowly off the apron and across the concrete to B-18, which led to the testing bay and take-off point on number five Runway.

"At 8:03 he started running up his four engines, and at 8:06 he informed A.T.C. that Flight 900 was ready for take-off and asked for clearance and changes. A.T.C. gave clearance for the take-off, announced there were no changes and that the requested altitude of 18,000 feet was cleared. Flight 900 left the ground at 8:09, one minute ahead of the flight plan schedule."

CHAPTER EIGHT

"MARJORIE CASSELL LOCHMAN, widow of Fred Lochman, was born in Los Angeles on April 26, 1929, the daughter of Joseph and Lora Cassell, both natives of California. Her father was a salesman for the wholesale grocery firm of Marcus Hochmeier Inc., and separated from her mother about seven months after her birth. He continued to support mother and daughter, under a decree of the California Supreme Court, until Marjorie's eighteenth birthday, when he

stopped sending monthly checks. He established residence in Mexico in 1940, marrying for the second time. Marjorie believes his wife is a Mexican national, daughter of a minor diplomat, but she was not certain.'

"Marjorie was educated in a Los Angeles elementary school and then attended Santa Monica High School when her mother moved to Santa Monica in 1934 to live as the common law wife of a Douglas Aircraft engineer by the name of John H. Whiteman. 'Uncle' John, with whom her mother had been having an affair since shortly after the departure of Joseph Cassell, was the only father Marjorie had ever known. He was outwardly a respectable professional man and churchgoer, but his sexual habits were not conventional, and there is a strong suspicion that he seduced Marjorie, when she was about fifteen. She was very reluctant to speak of this experience, and there is no way to judge whether she was telling the truth in the little she did tell, or whether she was dramatizing herself. She did recount with some vehemence, however, the alleged seduction of a boyfriend of hers by her 'Uncle' John, and she declared that this incident ended forever her relationship with her mother's lover. She called him a homosexual.

"There seems no question that Marjorie was and is unusually attractive to men and that she had a great many early sexual experiences.

"Marjorie took a nursing course at U.C.L.A. after her graduation from high school and at twenty applied for and obtained an appointment as a student hostess for Oceanic Airways. She attended the Oceanic hostess school for three months and became a junior hostess in May, 1950, shortly after her twenty-first birthday. She was popular with the airplane crews, with the possible exception of some of the other hostesses, and with many of the passengers as well. She made many friendships, and she never lacked dates at any of the Oceanic terminals, whether in America or abroad.

"Marjorie shared an apartment in Jackson Heights, Queens, with two other Oceanic hostesses up to the time of her marriage to Fred Lochman. She met Lochman at this apartment one summer afternoon

when he drove home from the airport with one of the other hostesses, Lorraine Barton, who had been in his crew from Paris. Lorraine was going to go out with Lochman to dinner and a show in New York, and he sat talking to Marjorie while he waited for her to get dressed.

"Marjorie mixed him a highball and talked to him for nearly an hour. At that time she was having an affair with a chemical engineer, she said, and her interest in Lochman was mild. However, she made a date with him for the next night, before he departed with Lorraine.

"She said she questioned Lorraine about him at length the next afternoon when she returned home, and Lorraine told her Lochman was an excellent lover, although when he drank he displayed fits of meanness and that once he had beaten her so severely that she couldn't sit down comfortably for days. Lorraine said she suspected Lochman was a sadist.

"The first time Marjorie went out with Lochman she refused to make love to him. She admitted this was difficult because, she said, she found he had a strong animal attraction for her. She phoned him the next morning and told him she had dreamed about him, but he was scheduled for a flight that day and had to forego the invitation inherent in her account of the dream. He wasn't back in New York for the next five days.

"Marjorie's first night with Lochman was violent, but satisfactory, she said, and it stirred in her such tremendous feeling that she forgot for a time every other man she had ever known. She said she thought she was in love at last, had made up her mind she was going to marry him.

"It took her three months to achieve Lochman. She described them as three miserable months for both because she sensed that her only certain weapon in this campaign would be denial. She said she never before had denied herself any sensual experience. But the end of it was their marriage, and she considered herself fortunate for several weeks.

"Twenty-five days after their marriage, Fred Lochman beat Marjorie so severely that she was taken to Queens General Hospital for treatment of multiple abrasions and contusions about the face and body. The official report was that she had been involved in an automobile collision.

"Marjorie said she never did have any feeling of constancy towards Lochman, despite the strength of her early love. She admitted she was violently jealous of him, and the thought that he might make love to another woman would send her into fits of rage. Their quarrels over her jealous accusations were constant, she said.

"Marjorie resumed her affair with the chemical engineer on the first flight Lochman took out of Idlewild after their marriage, which was nine days after the nuptials. She gave a variety of reasons for this. She said she felt that the engineer needed her; she said that she needed him, despite her love for Lochman; she said she never could be satisfied with one man; she said she returned to him only for companionship; she also said that he loved her more tenderly than any man she had ever known.

"The relationship between Lochman and Marjorie apparently started to deteriorate soon after their marriage and reached a climax in about eighteen months. This climax occurred over Lorraine Barton, and the scene was Marjorie's former apartment in Jackson Heights, which she had shared with Lorraine. Lochman had been due back from Paris on a Friday, but had switched flights with another captain who had become ill with undulant fever. He had arrived at Idlewild on Thursday instead. Lorraine was a hostess aboard this flight, and she had spent six hours of the night in a bunk with Lochman. Marjorie stated this as a fact but refused to say how she found out. Whoever her source of information, she went to the Jackson Heights apartment late Thursday night and entered with her own key, which she had never relinquished. She found Lochman sleeping beside Lorraine.

"A violent scene followed among the three, and Marjorie went back to Queens General Hospital with three fractured ribs and a broken nose, among other injuries. Lochman had told her, she said, that the reason he was sleeping with Lorraine was because she could not and never did satisfy him. Marjorie said it was then that she realized she hated Fred Lochman and had always hated him."

Calvin Colby stopped reading and shuffled his papers. "Apparently there was a great deal of ill will between these two," he said, "but there is nothing that would lead us to believe Marjorie Lochman would have attempted to get rid of her husband in such a fashion. There is no suspicion at this time against any employee or relative or friend of an employee of Oceanic Airlines."

"The passengers, then?"

"We expect that something of value will emerge about one of them."

"But you have nothing now?"

Colby shook his head. "Not what we want and need, Mr. Harrington."

"You mentioned two of the passengers you were already investigating at the time the plane disappeared—Aldo Vincenzi and Clarence Maiden. Has anything come of that?"

"Nothing that would connect either with the sabotage. We were hopeful about Maiden, and it is still possible, of course, that one of his many enemies may have placed the bomb aboard your airliner. Let me read you some of the report on Maiden's associates."

Colby picked out several stapled sheets from his file and began to read very quickly, skipping most of the detail.

"Principal opposition to Maiden's control of the A.C.D. (Amalgamated Chauffeurs and Drivers) comes from two groups: one within the union, led by Patsy Madrone and John Francis Kelley, known as Jingles; and the other the Waterfront District 23, controlled by the Brittan brothers, Frank and Don... The two attempts on Maiden's life seem to have originated in the fight of District 23 to take over Maiden's union... The attempt on Maiden's life last August by placing a dynamite bomb on the front porch of his home at Stony Point, just under his bedroom, was ordered by the Brittan brothers and engineered by Manny Holmann, now deceased. Holmann's body was found two weeks after the bombing incident in a stolen automobile on a street in the factory district of Newark, New Jersey. He had been shot in the head... Our witness, Howard Silver, who accompanied Holmann to the Maiden residence at the time the bomb was placed, has

disappeared and is believed dead... The income tax case against the Brittan brothers will be completed by the first week in January... Here's something of particular interest: *The bomb and timing device were assembled by Nat Covaleski, an explosives expert in World War II, who disappeared at the time Holmann was killed. Covaleski was married to Holmann's sister...* There's a lot of murder and violence there, Mr. Harrington."

"Yes, I see what you mean."

"But there is no evidence so far that the Brittans or any associate of theirs in District 23 had access to Maiden's baggage or to Flight 900. Covaleski has not yet been traced. So there is always that possibility, but it is very remote. I would say that Maiden's associates and enemies are poor prospects for us at this time."

"Not nearly as good as Fred Lochman's widow," said Harrington. "That girl worries me, somehow."

Colby shook his head. "No, forget her, Mr. Harrington. Her background is all wrong for this sort of thing. She doesn't in any respect fit the kind of person we're hunting for. She gained nothing from Fred Lochman's death except very nominal insurance. She already had her freedom from him; they've been separated for several months. No, she is not our type."

"You are hunting for a type, Mr. Colby?"

"Yes. I'll give you an example. Here's a report on a very likely couple." The FBI agent selected another file and began to read:

"Mr. and Mrs. Gordon Petrie, of Old Westbury, Long Island. Gordon is the son of Mrs. Franklyn Petrie, the former Elizabeth Fowler, by her first marriage to Lawrence Coxe Fowler. Young Fowler took the name of his stepfather following his mother's marriage to Petrie in 1932. Mrs. Gordon Petrie is the former Cora Walters, daughter of Harold Gosden Walters, the Long Island real estate operator who was killed ill all automobile accident in Florida in 1940.

"Gordon, an only child, was raised with much pomp by the household employees of the Fowlers, and following his mother's divorce and marriage soon thereafter to Petrie, he went away to school and spent very little time at home. He attended Exeter and Yale, as did his stepfather. He was expelled from Yale in his junior year as a result of the sequestering of several burlesque actresses in a men's dormitory following a fraternity dance.

"Gordon shortly thereafter went to work for Bethlehem Match, first as a salesman and later in the experimental laboratory. It was in the laboratory that he first revealed an original and inventive mind and a genuine flair for mechanics and chemistry. He enrolled in classes at Pratt Institute in Brooklyn, studying chemistry and engineering, and for the next year he gave all outward appearance of being serious and ambitious. Then came World War II, and he obtained a commission in the army as a lieutenant and went to the Mediterranean with a demolitions squad, distinguishing himself with his fellows in the campaign through Italy.

"Gordon met Cora Walters, then twenty-five, upon his return to America in December of 1944, during a thirty-day leave before he was to go to the Pacific theatre. They became acquainted at a U.S.O. dance and they appear to have spent the next three weeks constantly in each other's company, posing as man and wife. That is in their New York police record. On January 4, 1945, they were arrested at the Sutton East Hotel on a charge of attempted extortion and blackmail, and they were held in jail for twenty-four hours for lack of bail of $1,500 each. The complainant, one Hilton Fogarty of Brockton, Mass., suddenly withdrew the charges he had made and announced he would not appear against them as a witness. That ended the matter, and they were released, Gordon to go to the Pacific and Cora to retire to Florida to wait for him.

"The charges brought originally by Hilton Fogarty were that Cora Walters had enticed him into a room at the Hotel Sutton East, promising to make herself available to him, and that shortly after they had entered the room together and while they were both undressing,

76

Gordon Petrie had entered the room with a key of his own, announced Cora was his wife, and demanded $10,000 from Fogarty on the pain of exposure and public scandal. Fogarty was not frightened enough to permit the shakedown. He called the police. There is no record of why he withdrew the charges. Hilton Fogarty died two years ago.

"Gordon Petrie returned from the Pacific in August of 1946 with the rank of captain after having been in an army hospital of Lujon for six months with yellow jaundice and malaria, and went on inactive duty. He married Cora Walters in Florida the following month, and on October 12 both were once again under arrest in New York, this time charged with transporting stolen goods. The stolen goods were diamonds and other jewelry belonging to one Alice Wentworth Hanson of Coral Gables, Florida, part of the loot, valued at $350,000, stolen from her home the previous September 23. Gordon and Cora Petrie were not accused of having committed the robbery, although both had been guests of Mrs. Hanson at a dinner party the night the jewels vanished.

"The final disposition of this case is unusual. The New York police were induced to withdraw the charges against the Petries by both Mrs. Hanson and the insurance company. Mrs. Hanson swore that the Petries were acting for her as go-betweens for the return of the gems and the insurance company concurred in this, joining Mrs. Hanson in a refusal to aid in the prosecution.

"From that time until the present, Gordon and Cora Walters have kept their names out of police files, although not out of the newspapers. There are two later instances of jewel robberies during gatherings at homes of wealthy persons, where both Cora and Gordon had been guests and where both had been questioned along with other guests. There was no evidence presented in either case that they were in any way involved in the robberies.

"Cora Walters Petrie was raised on the fringes of New York society and attended the fashionable Miss Fincham's for two years. She left the school very suddenly towards the end of her second year. Two girls who were classmates said the reason for her departure resulted from her practice of climbing out her window and down the fire escape to attend parties until the early hours of the morning, then returning by the same means. One of these informants, a Mrs. William Harrow of Greenwich, Conn., described Cora as dashingly pretty, with a flair for clothes and men. (Not boys, she said.) Mrs. Harrow also declared that Cora drank heavily and smoked marihuana.

"Gordon and Cora Petrie appear to be the principal heirs to the Petrie estate, which is valued at this time in the neighborhood of $14,000,000. A breakdown of the Petrie assets and an analysis of the bequests to go to Gordon and Cora is in reports 10603 and 10604 of December 14.

"The relationship between the Franklyn Petries and their son and daughter-in-law is described as strained. The young Petries were seldom invited to the Sands Point home of the Franklyn Petries. Friends and servants at the Sands Point house report that there were many quarrels among the four, and that Gordon particularly aroused the animosity of his stepfather and mother through his continual extravagances and his debts.

"Both Gordon and Cora say they gave the Franklyn Petries Christmas presents before their departure since the elder couple were planning to be aboard for the holidays. Gordon says he and his wife gave his mother a cashmere sweater and a wristwatch and his stepfather a box of one hundred custom-made cigars, wrapped in packages that were marked, 'Not to be Opened Until Christmas.' Mrs. Franklyn Petrie's maid said that she saw two packages like those described by the Gordon Petries, and that Mrs. Franklyn Petrie packed both of them in one of her three bags.

The Gordon Petries have produced sales slips for a cashmere sweater and a wristwatch, and these purchases have been verified at the stores. There is no record of the box of cigars. Gordon Petrie says he bought them from a salesman who called at his home at Old Westbury. He says he had never seen the salesman before and does not know what company he represented. He says he threw away the receipt the salesman gave him."

CHAPTER NINE

NEWSPAPERMEN will tell you there is nothing deader than yesterday's newspaper or yesterday's news. They live in a world of the present and the events that compose the present. What happened yesterday is long gone—a bore.

It was Pete Morehouse's misfortune that he had never understood this or accepted it. When he had first become a cub reporter on the Press in 1923, after three years as an office boy, he had very quickly aroused the animosity of the city desk by following through to the dull and unreadable end each story to which he was assigned. He did it on his own time, to be sure, and he never relaxed his efforts on today's assignment so that he could follow through on yesterday's but the sheer weight of the memoranda and unprintable trivia that he turned in became a resented burden to the editors who selected the local copy.

It was a burden on Pete as well, but one that he assumed without resentment. The fact that he worked twice as long as anyone else was accepted by him as an inconvenience of the profession. Many years later, when Pete finally achieved a position on the city desk himself, and a twenty-five-dollars-a-week increase, he believed it was because of this tenacity and conscientiousness. He became even more tenacious, and each local story that developed was followed through by the reporters he assigned for day after dreary day.

This situation did not last long. There is a critical economic factor in the operation of any editorial department, and this caught up with Pete's practices in a very few weeks. There were just not enough reporters to cover the news in this fashion, and the staff could not be enlarged over a budgeted maximum. Pete was ordered to desist. And finally, when he attempted to circumvent this order, he was deprived of authority to give out assignments unless they were approved by the city editor.

Pete remained on the city desk occupied almost entirely with the routine chores of the nerve center of editorial operation. He kept the day book, a diary of all scheduled events throughout the city; he kept all of the books on expenses and hours worked; he audited and signed all expense accounts, the payroll, and salary advances; he negotiated with the Newspaper Guild on all minor complaints and adjustments; and he read copy on most of the brief items of news that were so vital for makeup purposes as fillers at the bottom of the pages and at the end of longer stories. He became known as the "short editor," and the fact that Pete was only five feet seven inches tall and slightly built gave an additional insinuation to this term that pleased the risibilities of many of his associates.

The truth is that Pete Morehouse was not taken seriously by his superiors as a newspaperman and as an assistant city editor. And the cream of the jest was his assignment finally to become head of the library, or morgue. It was never remembered or considered that some of the best reporters ever developed on the *Press*—such people as Cameron Hawkes and Bill Calson and Fran Addams and Jim Livermore—had all learned their basic art and, more important, their newspaper philosophy and newspaper morals, from Pete Morehouse.

Among the last persons on the *Press* who could have told you what made Pete tick—the whys and the wherefores of his preoccupation with yesterday's news and the bitter end of each story—was Pete himself. Pete was not articulate except when he sat down in front of a typewriter to compose an account of an event or the people involved in it, objectivity he had, complete and lucid. About himself or his feelings, he could tell you nothing.

The fact that by Wednesday, December 18, the story of the Oceanic airliner and her tragic end was dead distressed him deeply. He couldn't tell you why, but it did. He looked through the first edition of that day with a genuine feeling of loss of something important in his life that was missing. On an inside page he found an item of less than a hundred words recounting the fact that there were no new developments in the FBI investigation of the sabotage, nor were any arrests immediately in prospect. And even that item was missing from the following edition.

Pete hunted through the paper in vain for a follow-up story on Willard Gower. On Tuesday morning at 8:00 he had given Finley Browne a long memorandum on Gower, recounting everything he had found out about the purchase of the Atlantic City restaurant, what Erbe had been told by Mrs. Gower, and what Lawrence Keene had learned from Luke Wardell. He had laid the memo on Browne's desk while the latter was talking on the telephone, and he had waited until the city editor was finished.

Browne had glanced through the memo and had said, "Thanks Pete. I'll see what we can develop from this."

"It could turn out to be a hell of a story," Pete had replied.

"Yeah, yeah. We'll see."

Pete had stood there for a moment. He had wanted to say more, to tell Browne why he thought it would develop into a good story. Then suddenly he had realized that he didn't know why. All he had was a feeling, a hunch, and he had never tried to verbalize it. Now he discovered that he couldn't possibly put this into words that would have had any meaning to the city editor. He had turned abruptly and had gone to the stairway that led down to his own office.

But the wiretap story was still alive. Lawrence Keene was seeing to that. His entire column was devoted to the machinations of Hinemann and his associates, who had spied upon the rich and the powerful to steal their secrets and use them for their own gain. It was a good column, readable and explicit. Names were lacking, however—Pete felt that Larry could have mentioned a few of these who had benefited by the wiretap setup besides Hinemann, Wardell, Zannis, and Balthazar—but otherwise it was fine. But there was, again, no mention of Gower.

Pete got Larry Keene on the phone. "I was just reading your column," he said. "It's very good, believe me. But I was wondering why you didn't mention Gower."

"I may get around to him tomorrow," said Larry. "Frankly, he's not very important. He did the work and he got paid for it. He had no other interest in the tap; he didn't benefit from the information, as I see it."

"I don't know about that," said Pete. "His widow has bought an $82,000 restaurant at Atlantic City. She paid cash for it, too—all of it."

"I'm damned," exclaimed Larry. "Where'd you find that out?"

"From an Atlantic City paper that reported real estate transactions."

"Very interesting. What else?"

"Carl Yerbe went out to see Gower's widow the other day, and she told him she was buying the property for someone else."

"Who?"

"She wouldn't say."

"There'll be a record of that, probably. Well, in that case, it's not so much of a story, is it?"

"I don't know. I have a hunch about it. I have a feeling that—that, well, that Gower and Wardell and Zannis and

Balthazar are all tied up in some way with Lamar Hinemann's death on that airliner. I don't know how, but I think they are. I *feel* they are."

"You're seeing goblins, Pete. There's no connection there, you can be sure of that Hinemann's death has ruined the whole operation for all of them. Now they're in the soup, just because Hinemann didn't stay alive to take care of them. I know what I'm talking about, Pete. You're on the wrong track."

"I—I don't know. I keep thinking about it."

"Think about something else. This is open and shut. Wardell told me he's planning to marry Hinemann's widow, this Judy Starr person. Now I've known Wardell ever since we were kids together up on the West Side, and I know how his mind operates. He was doing all right with Hinemann. He was getting plenty of dough and he's got a fine house and he's living off the fat of the land. Suddenly his boss is dead. It's the end of the gravy train. So he makes the pitch for the widow, trying to recoup, trying to save what there is to save. But what's wrong with that picture is that Wardell hates women. He detests them, Pete, and the last thing in the world he ever would have done was to deliberately cut himself off from his fat income from Hinemann to marry Hinemann's widow—if she were all gold plated and set with emeralds. It's out of character for Luke Wardell; in fact, I'll give odds that he never marries this Judy."

"You could be wrong about Wardell, Larry."

"Sure. But I'm not. You know who tipped off the cops to raid the wiretap in the first place? Luke Wardell himself."

"Why would he do that, Larry?"

"He did. With Hinemann dead, he found himself completely out of the picture. And if he's out, everyone's out. He makes sure of that."

"Well, I guess you know what you're talking about."

"I do, Pete. Just forget Hinemann is in this plane sabotage."

At five minutes to noon Pete Morehouse got a telephone call from Cameron Hawkes.

"Do you want to meet me for lunch, Pete?"

"Sure. What's on your mind?"

"A promise is a promise. Besides, I need a look at your files. See you at Andre's in twenty minutes."

Over steaming bowls of minestrone Cam Hawkes told Pete about Colby's visit to Harrington. "This is nothing that can be published, he said. "But if you're working on the story, it may give you some leads. Personally I don't think it amounts to much, from your standpoint."

"No? Why not?"

"Well, what can you do with a confidential FBI report? You can't run a line of it or even refer to it. It's all libelous as hell until there are arrests and indictments. You can't even say that anyone of these people is being questioned or investigated. And I can't see you going out and giving the third degree to someone like Gordon Petrie and getting a confession from him."

"Gordon Petrie, eh? Isn't he Franklyn Petrie's adopted son?"

"That's the one. I'll let you read all this stuff, and then you can draw your own conclusions."

"You have copies of the reports?"

"Right here." Hawkes tapped his breast pocket. "They like my boss in Washington. They made up special summaries of their investigation for him."

"Is there one on Judy Hinemann?"

"Sure enough. Half a dozen pages."

"What does it amount to?"

"Not very much. You'll read it."

"Anybody connected with her?"

"Well, not directly with her. There's one on Vincent DiCastro."

"Who's Vincent DiCastro?"

"That was Lamar Hinemann's private secretary, major domo, man of all work."

"I haven't seen his name anywhere before."

"I've got a lot of names that will be new to you, people like Mona Coleman and Sylvester and Michelle Doble and Evan Brice Faulkner. You can read the reports but you can't do anything about them."

"Maybe not," said Pete. "You never know."

After a quick luncheon the two went to Pete's office and closed the door. Hawkes gave him the copies of the FBI reports, carbon copies typed on thin onionskin paper, and Pete read them through.

He found out about Gordon and Cora Petrie and their early troubles with the law and their debts.

He found out that Mona Coleman, apparently a famous fashion model whom he had not before heard of, was being kept in a luxurious apartment on Park Avenue by Baron Otto Vitello; that she and the Baron had had many bitter arguments before he left for Europe; that she did not expect him to return to her or to continue to support her.

He learned that Sylvester Doble, son of Henry Doble, had accused his father of having had an affair with his wife and that he had once threatened to kill him.

He discovered that Peggy Hart Coulardis was separated from Aristotle and that her attorneys were drawing up papers in an action seeking a settlement of several millions of dollars.

He learned that Evan Brice Faulkner and his mother, Martha Faulkner had been bitter enemies for several years and that she had recently refused to support him further unless he went to work, and that she had threatened to change her will to disinherit him. In connection with this, he learned also that Evan Brice had been arrested in 1947 on a charge of embezzlement from the brokerage firm where he was then employed and that his mother had made good the shortage of some $47,000.

He found out that Shirley Howe Manson and Louella Costello Manson, former and current wives of the playboy financier were actually aunt and niece and that Louella Costello disliked her husband and regretted her marriage to him.

Pete Morehouse learned all of these things, and he marveled at the deep troubles that seemed to dog the very wealthy. But he was not very much interested in these people and their troubles. What interested him was the report on Judy Starr Hinemann and, to a lesser degree, the report on Vincent DiCastro. He read these with the greatest concentration, and he made an effort to remember every salient detail.

About Judy Hinemann, he read:

Judith Lollar Hinemann (Judy Starr) was born in Atlantic City on March 28, 1930. Her father is George Lollar, operator of two ride concessions on the Steel Pier, Atlantic City, and her mother is the former Kate Starr, a performer in vaudeville and in cabarets in the twenties. Kate Starr has a police record in Atlantic City, Baltimore and Cincinnati for having been involved in indecent exhibitions and, in Cincinnati, for having contributed to the delinquency of a minor girl.

Judith Lollar attended public school and the Jefferson High School in Atlantic City for three years. She left high school in her third year due to pregnancy and shortly thereafter married a schoolmate, Arthur Winfield. The baby born four months later to Judith Winfield died after some fourteen hours due to a malformed pancreas. Upon her discharge from the hospital, Judith returned to the home of her parents, refusing further to live with her husband. The following year (1948) she got a job in the chorus of the Riviera nightclub on Broadway under the name of Judy Starr and lived for a year, up until the time of his death, with the manager of the club, Angelo Scotti. The murderer of Scotti has never been apprehended. His body was found in December of 1949 in a vacant lot in the Bath Beach section of Brooklyn. He had been shot through the heart. Judy Starr shortly thereafter became the mistress of Herman (Dutch) Froelich, a known gangster from Newark, N. J., who was among the four persons arrested and questioned in the death of Scotti. All were released by the New York police.

Judy Starr remained with Froelich for about six months, sharing a house with him at Miami Beach, Florida, until March of 1950, then removing with him to an apartment on Central Park South, New York City. She used the name of Mrs. Froelich and claimed at the time that they had been married in Florida. (Arthur Winfield, her first husband, had obtained a divorce from her on grounds of desertion the year before.) Judy Starr later denied she was ever married to Froelich, and there is no record of such a marriage. Now she denies that she ever lived with Froelich, or with Angelo Scotti, for that matter, but both of these episodes have been verified by others.

Following their separation, Froelich went to Los Angeles, presumably as the syndicate representative in that area, and lives luxuriously in Beverly Hills with no visible means of support. He is reported to be the gambling overlord of the West Coast (See 1733-A and B of April, 1951, and 8385 of June, 1953). Judy Starr remained in the Central Park South apartment that they had shared. The rental of this penthouse apartment in one of the new buildings was $750 per month. She had both a cook and a maid and sufficient funds for her living expenses on this scale. She dressed in the height of fashion and maintained charge accounts at a dozen of the city's most exclusive shops. She paid all of her bills promptly and with checks made out to her own account at the Madison National Bank. The bank records show monthly deposits to her account during this period of $2,500. These deposits were by check on the Northwestern National of Chicago and were signed by J. C. Finney, Trustee.

There is strong indication that Judy Starr was and still is being paid off by Froelich and by others, possibly because of some information vital to these persons that she had obtained and which she had passed on to some third party for safe keeping or, of course, for revelation in the event anything happened to her. The large sums she receives can be accounted for in no other way. Also, it is very unlikely that Froelich would have left her so peaceably unless she held some threat over him. He is known to have been deeply in love with her and to have vowed that he would kill any man who tried to take her away from him.

Judy Starr is one of the most sensationally beautiful girls ever to come to Broadway. She has a perfect figure, regular features, and no blemishes. She is an excellent dancer and is described by various choreographers for whom she worked as the ideal chorus girl. In addition, she is a bright and vivacious conversationalist, when she wants to be, and she has an easy, confident manner with men. She gives the impression of frankness and truthfulness even when it is known that she is lying. She is an almost impossibly difficult subject to interview. She will turn any conversation into intimate channels at will, and she does not hesitate to be seductive when she is seeking an advantage.

In the fall after her separation from Froelich, Judy Starr went back to the chorus, getting a job with a musical show scheduled for Broadway, "Babes in the Woods." The show played Philadelphia, Washington, and Boston, and on October 13 opened at the Morningside and played until the following June. She was popular among the members of the cast and the staff, although she spent most of her time offstage by herself and took part in very few activities with the others. She was not seen in the company of any men during this period. There is an indication that she met Lamar Hinemann while the show was in Washington.

She was still receiving her monthly checks from Chicago, and she kept her Central Park South apartment in New York, discharging her cook but retaining her maid. When the show closed in June, she went to Las Vegas with another girl, Sandy Shores, and after several weeks of gambling and sightseeing, the two girls joined the chorus at the Miramar Club. Dutch Froelich made several trips to Las Vegas during her stay there, but she declares she did not spend any time with him. She introduced him to the Shores girl and apparently promoted a friendship there, for shortly thereafter Sandy Shores went to Los Angeles with Froelich and moved into his Beverly Hills home as his housekeeper.

Judy Starr stayed in Las Vegas for three years, working at the Miramar and several other clubs. Meanwhile her monthly checks had been piling up in New York, and by the time she returned to the East she had a bank balance of $103,850. She moved into her Central Park South apartment, and she got a job immediately in the chorus at the Gay Paree. It was then that she started to appear in public with Lamar Hinemann.

Hinemann had an unsavory reputation and was not socially acceptable to any New Yorkers of his wealth or class, although he had developed a coterie more or less of his own of night club personalities and others on the fringes of society. (See reports 38507 A to G). So far as Judy Staff is concerned, Hinemann was not any more acceptable or presentable than Angelo Scotti or Dutch Froelich. It can be said that from this standpoint, he was the type of man that Judy seems to have been drawn to.

Little has been learned about their early relationship. Several persons who knew them both have stated that they first started to go around together while Judy was in "Babes in the Woods" in Washington, but it is not believed that they saw each other during the time she was in Las Vegas. There is no record that Hinemann visited Las Vegas during this period. Whether or not they shared an apartment or visited hotels together after she started seeing him regularly is not known. There is reason to believe that they spent some time together in the apartment of Vincent DiCastro, Hinemann's secretary, but DiCastro denies this, as do the employees of the building he then occupied on East 57th Street. It is certain that both were circumspect, which does not follow the prior pattern of either.

In August of 1955 Lamar Hinemann and Judy (Lollar-Winfield) Starr were married by a justice of the peace in Alexandria, Virginia, and boarded the liner Queen Mary the next day for a honeymoon on the

Riviera. They stayed at the Carleton Hotel in Cannes, occupying the royal suite for five weeks, then took a leisurely motor tour through France and Germany for the next three weeks. They returned to New York on October 2 and moved into the penthouse at 22 Sutton Place South, which Hinemann had purchased just prior to their marriage. They occupied three of the four penthouses on the twenty-third floor. Their own apartment comprised three bedrooms, living room, library, dining room, kitchen, and three baths, plus two large terraces. One small penthouse of three rooms was fixed up for Vincent DiCastro and another of four rooms for their servants, a butler, cook and two maids. The money for the penthouses—$78,000—came from Judy Starr's hoard at the Madison National, and the titles to the three apartments are in her name. Apparently in return for this, Mrs. Hinemann says she received upon her marriage 40,000 bearer bonds of Texas Exploration, which are worth $4,750,000 at today's market close. There is, however, no record of the transfer of these bonds to Judy Starr Hinemann, nor is there any record that Lamar Hinemann ever owned these bonds. Company records credit him with some 20,000 shares of common stock currently. He was chairman of the board of Texas Exploration upon his death. At the time of his marriage, he apparently held no shares in this company, under his own name. Mrs. Hinemann declared she would produce the bonds at any time it became necessary.

Judy Hinemann said that her husband decided very suddenly on December 4 that he would fly to Europe the next day. She declared that such sudden decisions were not unusual with him, that he often made up his mind on such matters at the last minute and that he would start out for Europe or South America or the West Coast with only a few hours' notice. She said that he pleaded with her to go with him but that she refused. She declared she was afraid to fly and that she did so only in the gravest emergencies.

The arrangements for the trip were made by Vincent DiCastro. He telephoned for the reservation, then later on Wednesday, December 4, went to the Oceanic offices and picked up the ticket.

Judy admitted that she and her husband have had quarrels during the past six or seven months. She declared she had become annoyed with his sexual extravagances and perversions and that she was well aware he was going to Paris principally to resume relationships with a woman friend. She said she expected him to be gone for a month at least, but that she was neither alarmed nor concerned. "He will come back to me," she said. "He always comes back to me." She refused to go into specific details about this matter or about her intimate relations with her husband. She declared she had learned to accept him as he was and there was no significance to their recent quarreling. She said that they quarreled no more than other married couples, and that they loved each other and had every intention of remaining married indefinitely.

Judy Hinemann said she had not given her husband a Christmas present before his departure nor had she placed one in his baggage. She explained that she had accounts at both Cartier's and Hermes in Paris and, if she were not angry with him by then, she would order presents for him by cable. She declared she didn't know what bags he took or what was in them. They were packed by the butler, Constantine, and by DiCastro, she said. This was the usual procedure with Hinemann's bags and was confirmed by both Constantine and DiCastro.

Judy would not comment upon other aspects of her personal life, beyond what is stated herein, nor would she admit that she had any particular men friends or had in any way, by thought or by deed, been unfaithful to her husband. Her attitude was not one of self-righteousness; she stated merely that sex did not interest her.

This appears to be somewhat out of character for Judy Starr.

CHAPTER TEN

THE REPORT on Vincent DiCastro was much shorter. It detailed his birth on the West Side in Chicago, son of a beer salesman for the Fuller Brewery, his schooling in the city's public schools, his two years at Northwestern, where he had received a substantial subsidy for playing football, and his departure from the university to join the marine corps in 1942. DiCastro's military record was not good. He had been on report a half a dozen times for various infractions, and he had been tried at a general court martial in 1944 for going A.W.O.L. at Toulon from the cruiser *Philadelphia,* for which he had served six months of a one-year sentence at Leavenworth Penitentiary. Some of the evidence given at the court martial was included, and this involved DiCastro with a black market operation in and around Toulon and Marseilles and linked him with one Julo Cassegrain, who was described as the black market chief in that area.

Upon his release from the penitentiary and his dishonorable discharge from the marine corps, DiCastro settled in New York and became associated with the firm of Cowles and Root, security brokers, as a salesman. The report went on:

This firm has been cited several times before the S.E.C. for bucket-shop methods and was investigated later and closed by the New York State attorney general. There is a strong suspicion that Sumner Cowles and R. Forest Root have evaded prosecution through bribery and influence.

Despite his prison record and his dishonorable discharge from the armed forces, Vincent DiCastro was welcomed into this firm, and within two years he became one of the junior executives. DiCastro seems to have displayed unusual ability in disposing of many of the issues offered by this company. He reported a gross income of $60,580 to the federal income tax bureau in 1948 and a gross income of $63,400 in 1949. In 1951 the firm of Cowles and Root was enjoined from further securities dealings by the New York State attorney general. DiCastro went to Florida and lived at Palm Beach until the end of March, 1952, then spent three months in Las Vegas, living at the Miramar. He says that he met Judy Starr there and was greatly attracted to her, but that she rebuffed him.

The report stated that DiCastro returned to New York in July of 1952 and met Lamar Hinemann at El Morocco the night of his return. He was introduced to Hinemann by Sumner Cowles. DiCastro at that time was broke as a result of losses and spending in Las Vegas, and he was seeking another job. He said that he and Hinemann hit it off immediately and that within three days he started to work for Hinemann as confidential secretary. He says that he told Hinemann of his Marine Corps record and his dishonorable discharge and that Hinemann made no comment. The report continued:

DiCastro refused to discuss his work for Hinemann, declaring that his position had been confidential and that he considered questions about it improper. He admitted that his position was more than that of a secretary and that he assisted Hinemann in many stock market transactions. He said that his personal relationship with the financier was most cordial and that after Hinemann's marriage to Judy Starr the three lived in harmony in their adjoining apartments on Sutton Place.

DiCastro remained reticent about his attitude towards Mrs. Hinemann. He declared that he admired her greatly and that there had never been anything more between them than a formal friendship. This may or may not be the truth. DiCastro is young, vigorous, and handsome, with an athletic figure, which he apparently takes care of. In contrast, Lamar Hinemann, fifteen years older than DiCastro, is short, overweight with a protruding stomach, and has very little hair on his head.

DiCastro confirmed the account given by Mrs. Hinemann of her husband's sudden decision to fly to Europe. He said that Lamar Hinemann notified him at 1:30 P.M. on December 4 of his desire to leave the following day and asked him to make reservations for him on the Oceanic flight, if possible. He said he was able to make the reservation immediately and two hours later picked up the ticket at the Oceanic offices. The following afternoon, he said, he packed two large bags with clothing and a small overnight bag with toilet articles and a razor. The large bags, he said, contained three business suits, a dinner jacket, a sports jacket, lounging robe, shirts, underwear, socks and handkerchiefs. He said that the butler Constantine helped him with both and could verify what was in them (The butler's verification has been obtained and will be found in 23587-c).

DiCastro gives the over-all impression of being inimical to this investigation and of withholding much information. This may be accounted for in part by the confidential position he held with Mr. Hinemann. However, in many instances, there seemed to be no logical reason for his reticence, considering that his employer is now dead.

DiCastro said he will remain in the Sutton Place apartment until all of the Hinemann affairs are finally settled and the estate distributed. He will work for Mrs. Hinemann in these matters, and his weekly salary of $350 will be paid by her, he said.

Pete Morehouse left a call at the city desk for Fran Addams, and when she came back to the office from an assignment at the Supreme Court covering the divorce hearing of the actress Corrine Shapley, she went to Pete's office.

"I've just read a summary of the FBI investigation of some of the people in this airplane sabotage," he told her. "You got pretty friendly with Judy Starr Hinemann, didn't you?"

"We hit it off fairly well after a while," Fran said. "She's not the kind of girl any other girl is going to get very friendly with, though. Maybe a man could."

"What do you think about her—I mean, really think?"

"I haven't given her much thought at all. I felt sorry for her, at first. She seemed to be lost...confused, I should say. I thought that the disappearance of her husband had tumbled her whole world down around her ears. Remember that no one knew what had happened to the plane when I talked to her. Then when she got to talking about Hinemann, I realized suddenly that she didn't like him at all, and that she didn't give a damn what had happened to him. That left me sort of swimming… I'd sum her up this way, Pete. She's a good actress. She isn't going to let anyone know what she feels and what she thinks unless she wants to. Does that answer your question?"

"Partly," said Pete. "You got time to talk? I'll send for some coffee."

"I've got to do an overnight on Corrine Shapley, and then I'm going to dinner with a brand new beau."

"Yeah? Anyone I know?"

"Cameron Hawkes."

"Cam? Say, that's news! So the boy wonder finally has discovered mousy little Fran Addams…"

"I'm not a mouse and you know it. All of this—severe hair, no makeup, loose clothes—it's my disguise, my working uniform."

"What happened, then?"

"I went to the A.N.P.A. ball last night at the Waldorf. Lori Vale, my roommate, fixed me up in one of her Hattie Carnegie creations, and I bowled 'em all over. Including Cam Hawkes."

"Cam is the wolf type," said Pete. "He's thirty-four or five now and he's never been married. The reason is that girls like him too much and are too generous with him so he doesn't have to marry them. You watch your step."

"*Phui.* What you don't know about boys and girls would bust open the seams of a public library."

"Well, I didn't expect you'd listen to me…I like Cam and there's no reason why you shouldn't. Just be careful."

"I repeat. *Phui.*"

"When are going to have time to see Judy Hinemann?"

"See her? What for?"

"Well—it's just an idea I have, Fran. I don't seem to be able to get rid of it. I keep thinking of Judy and the position she's in as a result of the death of her husband. You realize that little girl's going to have something like a hundred million dollars all of her own?"

"That's considerable. No, I hadn't been giving it any thought."

"Well, what's she going to do with it? Is she going to just sit up there in that penthouse all alone and count it over?"

"What do you think?"

"I think the first thing she's going to do is get herself a man. Somebody as different from Lamar Hinemann as she can find. Then I think she's going to have one grand smashing ball."

"So, suppose she does. What's the point?"

Pete shrugged. "I don't know, Fran. It's just an idea. Maybe something will come out. Maybe she'll tell you if she gets to like you. She's got to have somebody to talk to or she'll bust."

"Are you being vague on purpose? All right, I'll go up and see her again. I'll see if I can make an appointment with her for tomorrow evening."

"Thanks, Fran. And watch out for Cam Hawkes, hear?"

Pete Morehouse stood in front of the brownstone and looked at the worn, peeling face it presented to the world. There was a street lamp just to his left, and its light showed dirty white window sashes and grimy panes, a stoop cluttered with newspapers and dirt, and storm doors that sagged off their hinges. This was not at all what he had expected, and he felt a small resentment, mostly against himself, for having made the error of judgment.

He walked up the steps, avoiding a piece of torn newspaper that swirled in the wind, and went into the foyer, paved with dirty marble. To his left there were four mailboxes covered with scratched black paint and under them four pushbuttons with nameplates above them. The third from the left bore the name W. R. GOWER, printed in green ink on a grimy piece of cardboard. He pushed the bell under the name and then turned and held the brass doorknob on the inner door, waiting for the click of the electric latch. There was no click. He pushed the bell again.

A shadow suddenly appeared behind the pebbled glass of the door and the knob turned. The door opened a crack, and a pair of pale blue eyes in a wrinkled, unshaven face peered at him.

"I'm hunting for Mrs. Gower," Pete said.

"She ain't in."

"I'm from the Bureau of Internal Revenue, income tax department. When do you expect her?"

The door swung wide, and the man stood regarding him. He was dressed in baggy, striped pants, a dirty yellow shirt with dark perspiration marks under the arms, and frayed black suspenders. There were dirty brown carpet slippers on his feet.

"Government man, eh? You got identification?"

Pete tapped the briefcase in his left hand and said impatiently, "I am not concerned with you, my good man. I wish to see Mrs. Gower."

"Come in," he said.

Pete entered the hallway. It stank of cabbage and sweat and steam pipes. The man closed the door and started up the red-carpeted stairs.

"Follow me. She's on the second floor."

Pete followed his flapping slippers to a door on the floor above. The man knocked three times and called out, "Government man to see you, Mrs. Gower."

The door was opened immediately. Mrs. Gower was an unexpected contrast to these dingy surroundings. She was a neat looking, plump blonde woman in her late thirties. Her hair was short and recently curled, and her housedress of cotton was well cut and spotless. Her voice was deep and pleasant, "Government man?" she asked.

Pete nodded at her. "Internal revenue bureau, Mrs. Gower. I have a few questions I'd like to ask you about your current income tax."

"Come in," she said, swinging the door wide. Her brows were drawn together in a worried frown.

Pete entered into a brightly-papered hall, and Mrs. Gower closed the door. She led him to the front of the apartment, to an immaculate living room furnished with heavy, overstuffed chairs and a divan. There were two Klees on the wall above the fireplace, and he looked at them with interest. There was a glass-topped coffee table in front of the fireplace, and he strode to it and placed his briefcase on the glass, snapping it open and extracting several 1040 income tax forms and a pad of yellow, lined foolscap like that used by attorneys. Mrs. Gower watched him warily, standing by the divan.

"Sit down, Mrs. Gower," Pete said crisply, waving to the divan. "This will take only a few minutes."

Mrs. Gower sat on the divan. The worried frown was still on her face. Pete sat on the edge of an overstuffed chair and leaned over his papers, a pencil poised in his hand.

"We have received a report of a real estate transaction in Atlantic City, New Jersey, Mrs. Gower. An unusually large sum, all in cash, was involved. You paid $82,000 for a restaurant down there and—"

"It was a check," she interrupted. "I paid by check, not cash."

"Well, it's the same thing. Now, Mrs. Gower, we want to know where you got that money."

She looked at him and bit her lower lip. "Do I have to tell?" she asked.

Pete nodded at her. "Of course, Mrs. Gower. It is required by government regulations."

"You will not tell anybody?"

"No, I would have no reason to tell anyone. Your tax return is a public record, however, and can be examined by others."

She sat silent for a moment, her eyes cast down. "Some of it I got from my husband," she said. "He was killed two weeks ago. You know about that?"

"Yes, we know about that."

"Most of the money, $70,000, comes from my business partner, Mr. Aganna."

"Mr. Aganna?"

"Yes."

"Who is he?"

"He is—my partner."

"I mean, what is his full name and his address?"

"Constantine Aganna. He lives in Manhattan. I do not know his address."

"You do not know his address? Isn't that very peculiar, Mrs. Gower?"

"No. He comes here. I see him when he comes here."

"I will have to know more about him," said Pete severely.

"If you will wait here a little while, my brother will be here. He can tell you. He knows all about Mr. Aganna."

"I haven't much time, Mrs. Gower. Who is your brother?"

"He is Kurt Erhardt. He has a radio and television shop in Manhattan, on Nassau Street. My husband was his business partner."

Pete Morehouse suddenly felt very uneasy. He remembered Fran Addams' description of Kurt Erhardt—a big, tough character. He stuffed the papers in his briefcase and snapped it shut.

"I'll see your brother another time," he said, getting up. "What is his address?"

"His store is at 116½ Nassau Street."

Pete strode purposefully towards the door. He felt that he had to get out of this place quickly. He regretted the foolish impulse that had led him to pose as an internal revenue man. There was danger in it, and not only the danger of arrest for impersonation.

"You won't wait for my brother?" Mrs. Gower asked as Pete put his hand on the doorknob.

"I haven't got time this evening," he replied. As he turned the knob, the door was suddenly thrust inward, and he had to step aside quickly to keep from being bowled over. He stood looking at a tall, hard-faced man of forty-odd with, china-blue eyes and hair bristling in a crew cut.

"Who is this?" the man demanded, shifting his gaze to Mrs. Gower.

"Oh Kurt," she replied. "I was hoping you'd come. This man is from the income tax."

"Yeah?" He fixed Pete with a grim stare. "What do you want?"

"Mrs. Gower will explain it to you," said Pete in as firm a voice as he could muster. "Now if you will excuse me…"

He attempted to brush by the big man, but he suddenly found himself wedged against the doorsill.

"Tell me what you want?" demanded Kurt.

There was something suddenly ridiculous about the situation, and Pete looked up into the hard face and smiled. He realized there was no reason for the panic he had felt because of his guilt over the impersonation. "There is a severe penalty for assaulting an employee of the Internal Revenue Bureau," he said with assurance.

His manner, if not his words, was effective. Kurt stepped away from him and regarded him uncertainly. Then he looked at his sister. "What did he want to know?" he asked her.

"I'll see you in your shop at Nassau Street," said Pete, moving towards the stairway. Then he turned and shook an admonitory finger at the big man. "I'll expect you to tell the truth," he said.

CHAPTER ELEVEN

THE MAN'S BODY was lying crosswise on the large double bunk to the right of the door as you entered the stateroom. There was a bullet hole and a smear of blood on his right temple. There was a pool of blood under his head and a splatter of it on the surrounding blanket. His right arm was raised, and near the grey-white fingers of his right hand resting on the blanket was a Luger pistol.

Detective Second Grade Howard O'Malley of Brooklyn headquarters was questioning the room steward and the first officer, who stood just inside the door of the stateroom. He was making notes in a black notebook with a frayed leather cover.

"What time was that?" he asked the room steward, a short, dark man of thirty, who spoke English with a slight Norwegian accent.

"A little after eleven. I knocked on his door. There was no answer. It was open so I came in. He was like that." He motioned towards the body with his hand.

"You didn't hear a shot?"

"No."

O'Malley turned to the first officer. "When did you get here?"

"The steward came for me. It was 11:09. I was in my office on the next deck, signing the manifests. I came right down with him, and he showed me the dead man. I tried to find a pulse on his left wrist, but there was none. I saw the note over there on the desk. Then I notified the captain and I went down to the pier and telephoned the police."

"You hear a shot?" O'Malley asked.

The first officer shook his head. "No. The winches were running on the forward deck, loading the last of the cargo. Two automobiles. They make a lot of noise."

"You didn't shoot him?" O'Malley asked.

"No. I didn't shoot him."

O'Malley shrugged and turned back to the steward. "What time was it these two men left?"

"It was some time before I came to knock on the door. They had been waiting for Mr. Aganna since nine. Mr. Aganna came aboard a little before ten. I helped him with his bags. The men had been waiting in the lounge. That's just next door. They came into the cabin here just as I was leaving. They came in and they closed the door and I thought they locked it. I didn't see them leave."

"You get a look at them?"

"Well—yes. They were about the same height about two or three inches taller than I am. I'd say about five feet ten or eleven. They had on dark blue coats and dark grey hats. Both the same. They looked alike, I guess. They didn't take their hats off."

O'Malley regarded the steward with dislike. "You got a look at 'em, eh? One of 'em was a Siamese in a yellow kimono, and the other was an Egyptian belly dancer in drag... O.K." He turned to his partner, who was filling out an official report at the writing desk. "You got everything you need, George?"

Detective Third Grade George Farrell nodded. "Where the hell's the doc?" he asked.

O'Malley motioned with his hand to the steward and the first officer. "You can go," he said. Then he turned back to Farrell. "What do you make of this, George?"

"He knocked himself off," said Farrell.

"Maybe. Maybe not. That note looks phony to me. I got a hunch about it that's all."

Farrell picked up a sheet of notepaper with an imprint embossed in blue ink in the right-hand corner—*S. S. Comstock*. "What's wrong with it?"

O'Malley took the note from Farrell's hand and read it, *"There's nothing to live for. Constantine Aganna."* He shook his head. "This guy Aganna was going back to the old country, probably the first time since he came to America. He's got dough. Look at his clothes. There's $3,000 in his money belt. He buys a ticket on this here boat and he comes on board an hour before it's to sail. Then he sits down and he writes himself a note and he knocks himself off. No, George, it don't add up. Them hoodlums who was waiting for him shot him and wrote the note. I got ten dollars says that's the way it was."

"Maybe," said Farrell. "I wonder what the hell's keeping the doc?"

"When he gets here, we go hunting for them two monkeys," said O'Malley.

"O.K. I got nothing else to do tonight."

"You're damned right you haven't," said O'Malley.

Fran Addams sat in a corner of the pink divan with her feet curled under her, sipping Scotch and soda. She didn't like the color of the divan and so she felt uncomfortable on it. Nor did she like the huge coffee table in front of her, a slab of two-inch glass in the shape of a kidney resting on a tripod of thick branches that were finished to look like driftwood. She glanced at it with distaste, then looked slowly around the rest of the room, heavy with expensive luxury. She was reminded of a room in a museum. It was cold and unlived in. There was no piece of furniture in it, no picture or drape that beckoned to you, that said to you, "Be comfortable with me." The only warming thing in the whole room was the glass in her hand. She raised it to her lips again.

Then Judy Hinemann came back in and sat in the pale green chair on the other side of the coffee table. "Melissa will make us some hors d'oeuvres," she said. "I'm famished."

"You want to go out to dinner now?" asked Fran.

"No, not out. Won't you have dinner with me here?"

"But *I* invited *you* to have dinner with me."

"I don't think it would be a good idea. Let's have dinner here. Melissa can really cook up a storm."

"All right, Judy... You haven't been out of this apartment since December 5, have you?"

Judy shook her head. "No."

"You afraid of something?"

Judy laughed. It seemed to be a genuine laugh. It lit her face, especially her eyes, and you could see the vivacity that gave her beauty so much meaning. In repose, she had a rather serious inward look, and it was easy to imagine much mystery behind her green eyes. When she laughed, she was gay and pixyish and there was a different kind of promise in her.

"There's nothing to be afraid of," she said.

"Well, I just wondered."

"I haven't thanked you for that wonderful story you wrote about me," she said. "You made me sound so—intelligent."

"You're not a dumb blonde, you know."

"Maybe not in some ways," she said.

"But somehow I just can't imagine your staying alone in this apartment day after day, night after night."

"I have friends," said Judy. "I'm not always alone."

"That's good. When you're alone, you're liable to think too much."

"I've got nothing to think about."

"Your husband?"

"Lamar? No, I don't think about him."

"You don't miss him?"

Judy pondered this, her brows puckered. "Yes, I guess I do, in a way. I got fairly used to him in two years, I guess he became a sort of habit. It'll take time before I get over the habit."

"You going to marry again, Judy?"

"Certainly not. Why should I get married? I've got everything I could possibly need."

"Except a man."

"I can always get plenty of those. A man—just a man—is the easiest thing in the world for a girl to get. But I suppose I am hunting for somebody special. I guess I've been hunting for him all my life. The trouble is, I don't know just exactly what I want in a man. I've found out a lot about what it *isn't*, but I haven't found out what it *is.*"

"It wouldn't be a father for your children, would it?"

Judy laughed again. "I'm not the mother type," she said.

"All women are the mother type."

"That's not for me," said Judy with conviction. "I've tried it."

"Well, that's one thing you are afraid of then," said Fran.

Judy looked at her for a long time before she replied. "Maybe," she said finally.

Fran said, "I'm going to get married. I've found a man who will be the father of my children."

"You're in love," said Judy. "That's all that amounts to."

"No. I've been in love before, but it was never like this. I've just discovered it."

"Does he know it yet?"

"Not a suspicion. I'll let him in on it, a little at a time."

"Make this part of it last," said Judy. "It's the best part."

"I'll do that." Fran finished her drink and waited. Sooner or later, Judy would open up, she felt certain, if she could just keep the subject on men.

The two girls had dinner in the large dining room, another room that was cold and unfriendly to Fran Addams. Melissa, a Negress of stern, uncomprising mein, served vichyssoise, broiled chicken breasts, salad and coffee. Judy talked a little about men she had known, recounting disconnected and humorless incidents and describing their pursuit of her and the lengths to which they went to achieve her. She had all of the frank, unabashed egotism and hypocrisy of the beautiful girl who uses her beauty as her single weapon. Fran found it very dull talk, and she realized with a sense of frustration as the hours passed that she was learning nothing of any use to Pete Morehouse or, as far as that went, to any newspaper.

At 10:30 Judy looked at her watch and jumped from her chair in the living room in alarm. "I had no idea it was so late," she said. "I hope you will forgive me, Fran dear, but I must ask you to go. I—well—I have a sort of appointment."

Fran nodded and got up. She followed Judy to the foyer and put on her coat. Then she took Judy's hand and she said, "I've had a wonderful evening, Judy. I hope we can do this again."

Judy was nervous, distraught. She moved towards the door. "Sure, Fran. Look, call me, will you? I'm sorry to have to rush you off this way."

Then there was the noise of a key in the lock, and the door opened. A man came striding into the foyer. He was tall, with an athletic build, dark, wavy hair and shining hazel eyes. His lips were loose and too pink for a man's. But the over-all impression he gave was that of handsome virility. He looked at Fran Addams with unconcealed surprise. He wore a maroon silk lounging robe over a white shirt that was open at the throat and patent leather slippers.

"This is Fran Addams," said Judy, giving her a brief unfriendly glance. "Vincent DiCastro, my husband's secretary."

"How do you do?" said Fran. "I was just leaving."

"Don't leave on my account," said DiCastro easily. "I was just checking on Mrs. Hinemann to make sure she was all right before I go out on my nightly prowl in the bistros."

Judy nodded. "He looks after me like a mother hen," she said.

"Well, I'll be going," said Fran.

"Good night, dear," said Judy.

DiCastro held the door open for her, and she stepped into the hall. Then he followed her to the elevator after closing Judy's door and pushed the button for her.

"Thanks," said Fran.

She felt him looking her over. Tonight her hair was curled, and she wore a smart navy wool dress from Bergdorf's. She knew how to dress all right, when there was a sufficient reason for it. This navy dress showed a figure that was every bit as good as Judy's.

"You're the newspaper girl, aren't you?" DiCastro asked.

"I'm on the *Press,*" she replied.

"You wrote that story about Judy—Mrs. Hinemann?"

"Yes."

"It was a lousy story. You keep away from Mrs. Hinemann. You write anything more about her and I'll make trouble for you."

"I'm sure you will," said Fran as the elevator arrived and the door slid open. "Good night, Mr. DiCastro."

Pete Morehouse bought a *Times* and a *Tribune* from Joe Boyle, as was his custom, dropping the coins into the outstretched hand of the blind news dealer, saying, "Good morning, Joe," and he glanced at the headlines as he walked slowly to the station platform. There, he divided his time between reading the front page of the *Times* and returning the greetings of a dozen or so of his neighbors. When the train rumbled to a stop, he got into the second car and found a seat near the door next to a plump, middle-aged woman who breathed loudly, as though she were suffering from asthma, and wore an offensive perfume. The consciousness of her breathing and her perfume was not insistent enough to distract Pete from his newspapers, and he started to read quickly and thoroughly.

As the train began to slow down for Jamaica he was reading with more than passing interest a story on page 14 of the *Times* headed:

HINEMANN BUTLER DEAD
Body of Servant Found on Ship,
Believed to be Suicide

The story read:

The body of Constantine Aganna, 48 years old, butler in the employ of the late Lamar Hinemann, financier who was lost on the New York-Paris Airliner of Oceanic Airways December 5, was found at 11 o'clock last night in his stateroom aboard the S.S. Comstock at Pier 47, Brooklyn. Mr. Aganna had been shot through the head and police reported the death as probable suicide.

Police stated that a Luger pistol was found near Mr. Aganna's right hand and that a note, apparently in his handwriting, was found on the writing desk in his cabin. Deputy Inspector George DeWitt of Brooklyn headquarters said there were several puzzling aspects to the case and that it was still being investigated. Two men visitors who left

Mr. Aganna's cabin some time before the body was discovered, are being sought for questioning, said Mr. DeWitt.

Mr. Aganna, a native of Turkey, had engaged passage on the Comstock, a freighter with accommodations for twelve passengers, to Istanbul. The sailing of the ship was delayed for one hour while police questioned officers and crewmembers. The body of Mr. Aganna was removed to the Kings County Morgue.

The train had stopped and Pete looked up at the influx of commuters who were jamming into the aisle and who would ride the rest of the way into the city in the greatest discomfort. He had a strong impulse to get off the train and seek a telephone, to tell Finley Browne what he knew and what he suspected about Constantine Aganna.

Then he realized that he didn't know very much and that his suspicions were as yet unconfirmed—that if he did phone Browne, he would only make a fool of himself once more and earn the contempt of the city editor. He folded up the *Times* and opened the *Tribune* to hunt for the story about Aganna there.

He found it on page two. The *Tribune* story quoted the note: *"There's nothing to live for. Constantine Aganna."* It also gave Mr. Aganna's address as 1537 Sterling Place, Brooklyn. And that, as Pete Morehouse knew very well, was also the address of Mildred Gower and the late Willard Gower.

CHAPTER TWELVE

AT 4:10 P.M. on Friday, December 20, which was fifteen days after the loss of Flight 900 and her rich cargo, Pete Morehouse lowered himself into a chair beside the desk of Finley Browne, city editor of the *Press*. The last regular edition of the day had gone to press ten minutes before, and the pressure of the deadlines was off. Browne, a rangy

Lincoln of a man with a deeply lined face and a mop of grey hair that always seemed to need combing, was tilted back in his chair with his left foot on the edge of the desk, smoking a cigarette and reading a copy of *Editor and Publisher*. He was reading the want ads in the back, studying the jobs that were open on country newspapers. Like most metropolitan newspapermen, he had a dream of retiring one day to a quiet, peaceful paper where there was only one deadline a week and no ulcers. He glanced up at Pete and waited for the head of the *Press* library to speak.

Pete had prepared for this interview for several hours. He had written a ten-page report, a complete summary of everything he had learned about Judy Hinemann, Willard Gower, Mrs. Gower, Constantine Aganna, Vincent DiCastro, Kurt Erhardt, Luke Wardell, Morton Zannis and Louis Balthazar. He had reviewed all of the facts he had collected and arranged them logically, then considered the arguments and the deductions he would present—if Finley Browne would listen to him. If not, of course…

"I don't want to take up too much of your time, Finney, but I've got something here that's very important. Will you read it?"

Pete handed the city editor his report, neatly typed on copy paper. Browne took it in his hand, weighed it, and said, "Do I have to?"

He grimaced at the stricken look on Pete's face and started to read. He spent no more than thirty seconds on the first page—this was about Willard Gower and his death—and was galloping through the second when, down at the bottom, a paragraph caught his eye. He read it a second time. The paragraph said:

This ties up Willard Gower to Morton Zannis, Louis Balthazar and Luke Wardell, and through Wardell to Lamar Hinemann and Mrs. Hinemann. The other connection is through Willard's widow,

Mildred Gower. Mrs. Gower on Monday paid $82,000 in cash for the Elite restaurant on the Boardwalk, Atlantic City. She received $70,000 of this sum from Constantine Aganna, who was Lamar Hinemann's butler. Aganna's body was found in his stateroom on a freighter in Brooklyn Wednesday night. He was shot through the head. Two men had visited him earlier. Their descriptions are similar to the two men who ran up the stairs at Chambers Street after Gower was killed.

Browne looked up at Pete and frowned. "You gave me a memo about some of this, didn't you?"

"Yes."

"There was nothing about the Hinemanns in it."

"I just found that out. I've been working on it."

Browne continued to read. On page six he came to another paragraph that arrested his attention. "Where'd you get this stuff on Judy Hinemann?"

"Fran Addams went up to see her."

"Fran, eh? You still giving out assignments to my staff?"

Pete's face turned red. "No, Finley. Honestly. She offered to do it on her own time."

Browne laughed. "Stop acting like a rabbit." He read the paragraph aloud. *"Luke Wardell says he will marry Judy Hinemann in six months. He told this in strictest confidence to Larry Keene. However, shortly after 10:00 P.M. on December 18 Vincent DiCastro entered Mrs. Hinemann's apartment with his own key. This was at a moment when Judy was trying to hurry out a visitor, after telling the visitor she had an appointment. DiCastro wore a dressing gown over trousers and shirt. His apartment adjoins that of Mrs. Hinemann."*

Pete said, "That was Fran Addams."

Browne nodded and went back to his reading. He finished the rest of the report quickly and tossed it on his desk by his foot. "Well?" he said.

"Well—what do you think?"

"I suppose the point you're trying to make is that one of these people dumped that airliner in the ocean. Is that it?"

"Yes. That's what I think."

Browne took his foot off his desk and came forward in his chair, his face close to Pete's. He said, "You've collected a lot of circumstantial evidence against these people that sounds like some half-baked mystery story. You've got ten pages of innuendo and suspicion—" he slapped Pete's report with his hand—"and not enough concrete evidence to put in your eye. There are experts working on this airliner sabotage, an organization of some ability and repute called the FBI. Let me read you something the FBI is working on just to give you an idea. Bill Cornish picked it up this morning."

Browne took a bunch of keys out of his pocket and unlocked his top left-hand drawer. He took out a couple of sheets of copy paper and started reading. *This is the confidential report from Colby, agent in charge here. Colby says that he is confident there will be a break in this case very shortly. FBI has been questioning Evan Brice Faulkner for past four days and have been checking all of his movements on December 4 and December 5 and prior. Here is summary of case against Faulkner: He and mother quarreled often. Mother had threatened to disinherit him and undoubtedly would have upon return to America on December 21. She had appointment with her attorneys Coldwell and Brian, on December 22 to discuss changes in her will. Faulkner owes more than $15,000 at this time, a chunk of $8,200 of it to gamblers Marty Greene and Sam Elwell. Faulkner has promised to pay Green and Elwell before first of year.*

"Faulkner has $25,000 worth of insurance on his mother that he admits he persuaded her to take out in the quarter insurance machines at the airport before plane took off.

"Faulkner was with his mother on December 5 when her two bags were packed. He says bags were packed by two maids and that he did not have access to them. Maids say Faulkner did have access to bags,

that they were in hallway of apartment for an hour before being taken downstairs to car by chauffeur and that during this hour Faulkner was alone in living room, just off hallway, while his mother and maids were in bedroom."

"Faulkner served two years in the army in the signal corps, and, he has a working knowledge of electricity, of timing devices and of explosives. His knowledge is considered sufficient for him to have constructed a time bomb out of dynamite and a timer. However, the FBI says there is no evidence linking Faulkner with the purchase of any material with which to make such a device. It is the total lack of such evidence that has forestalled Faulkner's arrest.

"Colby told me Faulkner appears to be in a highly nervous state and contradicts himself in many details from day to day. He is not cooperative or frank.

"It is Colby's opinion that Faulkner will not confess until they are able to confront him with concrete evidence linking him to the time bomb and its manufacture. The FBI is now concentrating all of its efforts along that line, and they are confident of success. Colby told me, 'It is only a matter of time now.'—CORNISH."

Browne put the report away and locked the drawer. He said, "That's the status of the investigation of the sabotage of the Oceanic plane as of today. Stop wasting your time."

Pete nodded his head and got up. All the carefully planned arguments that he had been arranging and polishing were fled. There just wasn't anything more he could say to Browne that would convince him, in the face of Bill Cornish's report. He knew this, and yet...

"That's still not the last word—not until they arrest and indict this Faulkner." Pete felt dismayed and ashamed that he should have stood there and continued to argue. What he should have done was to leave and say nothing. But it was not in Pete's nature to let anything go, to give up on any idea that he considered valid, and he just would not heed his better judgment and the urgings of his reason. "I'll give you ten to one they never indict Faulkner."

"All right, Pete. You know more than the FBI," said Browne wearily. "Meanwhile, let's police up the morgue and not lose so many pictures and cuts, eh?"

"Sure," said Pete. "Whatever you say."

The trial of Luke Wardell, Morton Zannis and Louis Balthazar for eavesdropping, a crime against the peace and dignity of the People of the State of New York, maximum penalty two years' imprisonment, came up on Monday, December 23, at 9:00 A.M. before Judges Graham, Mueller and Ottman in Special Sessions, with Judge Graham presiding and without a jury. The trial got under way several minutes after nine, with Assistant District Attorney Martin Jacobson representing the People and Barron Eastman appearing for the defendants. The first motion made was by Eastman, a roly-poly little man with a cherubic face, who was piling up a record of successful criminal defenses that bade fair to put Steuer and Liebowitz in the shade. Eastman's motion was for a severance for Luke Wardell, and he presented this to the court in the form of an affidavit followed with oral argument. The brunt of his argument was that Wardell, acting as attorney for the Fifth Avenue Recording Company and for Morton Zannis and Louis Balthazar, was not to be implicated in the alleged crimes of his clients nor in any way accused with them for their alleged misdeeds; that he was, in fact, unaware of the existence of the wiretap or the purposes for which it was allegedly used.

Martin Jacobson opposed the motion, stating that he would prove Wardell was an active participant in the wiretap operation and that, in fact, he alone, and not Zannis or Balthazar, had had it installed and had dictated its operation.

"There is no question in our minds that Mr. Wardell is the brains of this entire setup, and we shall produce a witness, in a unique position to know all of the details of this operation, who will testify to that effect. It would be a grave error to permit a severance and the resulting doubling of the expenses to the People in this action, which is in essence a simple conspiracy among these three defendants to eavesdrop for personal gain and to the detriment of their victims."

The three judges held a whispered conference, and then Judge Graham said, "The court is strongly inclined to grant this motion, for a principle involved here—that an attorney's relationship to his clients is normally paramount. However, the prosecution clearly intends to seek to implicate this defendant with the conspiracy. The charges in the indictment do not in any sense differentiate the actions of this defendant from those of the other two, nor does the circumstance of his position as attorney for these two defendants and for the company appear to mitigate in any way his responsibilities for his actions. Motion denied."

As Judge Graham pronounced his ruling, the courtroom door opened, and Pete Morehouse and Larry Keene came in and walked down the aisle between the almost empty seats— there were fewer than a dozen spectators—and to the press table to the left of the bench. They passed behind the three defendants at their table, and Luke Wardell turned and spoke a greeting to Larry. They sat beside George Ashfelder of City News, who was the only reporter covering the trial. Since City News covered for all of the newspapers, no other reporters had been assigned. The trial was not considered to be important enough for any of the Specialists who gave blow-by-blow accounts of the more sensational court actions. Nobody was really interested in Luke Wardell and Morton Zannis and Louis Balthazar, outside of Larry Keene, for his column, and Pete Morehouse. Pete, of course, was not even a reporter. But he was there anyway.

Larry asked Ashfelder, "What happened?"

"Wardell asked for a severance. Motion denied."

The first witnesses were called. Deputy Inspector Charles O'Hare described in the stilted language of police reports the circumstances of the raid upon the suite of offices on the second floor of the Lackey Building and exactly what and whom he and his men had found. Jacobson led him expertly through his account, omitting no salient details. O'Hare gave a full description of the equipment and told exactly how he and Detectives Walter Janney and Phillip Hesterberg, police department communications experts, had traced the lead-in cable from this equipment to the basement of the building, through which passed the telephone trunk cables of three East Side telephone exchanges. Inspector O'Hare was on the stand for nearly an hour before he completed his testimony.

Barron Eastman, on cross-examination, asked him only one question. This question was whether the referred-to trunk cables of the telephone company had been in any way cut or defaced or altered, and whether, as a result of this cutting or defacing or altering of insulation or any physical covering, an electrical connection had been made that led to the rooms in which had been found the recording and other electronic equipment.

The inspector attempted to explain, and Eastman cut him off short by demanding a yes or no answer. "Either these cables were cut or defaced in some way so that an electrical connection was made, or they were not," he said. "What is your answer, inspector. Yes or No?"

"No," said the inspector.

Jacobson quickly established on re-direct examination of the inspector that telephone wires could be tapped by indication as well as by direct connection; that all modern equipment used this principle, and that the direct-connection method was obsolete. Eastman paid no attention to any of this, holding a whispered conference with his three clients.

Janney and Hesterberg followed O'Hare to the stand and corroborated in every detail the inspector's testimony. On cross-examination they both answered "no" to Eastman's single question, which was the same one he had asked O'Hare.

The court was then recessed for luncheon, and Pete Morehouse and Larry Keene went into Judge Graham's chambers and talked to him while he changed from his robe to his suit jacket. Larry knew him well and called him Bob.

Larry asked, "What do you think, Bob?"

The judge shook his head. "It's open and shut," he said. "They're as guilty as Cain, but they're going to get off on that technicality."

"About the electrical connection?" asked Pete.

Judge Chambers nodded. "The law is very explicit. It specifies an electrical connection. There is nothing in it about induction or about any other possible method of tapping a telephone or overhearing a telephone conversation. It's an eavesdropping law, so-called, and yet it concerns itself with only this single form of eavesdropping, to wit, making a physical electrical connection with another person's telephone, not your own. Any other kind of device that would enable a person to overhear a telephone conversation is exempt. That is the full implication of the law, as it is written. What we need is a new law. There is a good federal law that covers wiretapping, so perhaps we should rely upon a federal indictment."

"What will you do, find them not guilty?" asked Larry.

"No, not unless they produce some very unexpected defense, and I can't imagine what that could be. There is a good chance, of course, that Luke Wardell will get off. I don't know how Jacobson expects to tie him in with the operations of Zannis and Balthazar, but I'd bet on Luke if I were a betting man. Let's say that Luke will be found not guilty. Then we'll convict the other two and let the appellate division reverse us on the technicality. I say, let them decide it, not us."

During luncheon with Larry and Judge Graham at the Courthouse Grill across Foley Square, Pete told them most of what he had found out about the three in the wiretap case and their connection with the Hinemanns and Willard and Martha Gower. The judge listened carefully while he ate, and after Pete had topped off his account with the death of Constantine Aganna, he looked at Pete and scowled.

"Who knows about all this?" he asked.

"A few of us on the *Press*, nobody else. Of course, some of it has been published in the newspapers."

"I know. I read about Aganna—about Gower, too. But you've tied 'em all up very nicely, Pete. What are you going to do about it?"

Pete shrugged. "There's nothing I *can* do. I'm not even a reporter any more. The *Press* isn't interested. Nobody is."

"You know Gordon Buell?" asked Judge Graham.

"Slightly," replied Pete. "I've met him a couple of times."

"I'll make an appointment for you to see Buell. He's your man on this. When can you see him?"

"Any time after five—today, tomorrow."

"I'll try to make it today. You coming back to the trial?"

"Sure," said Pete. "We hear Jacobson's got some fireworks."

"Fireworks?" asked the judge.

"He's going to spring a surprise witness," said Larry.

"I hope so," said the judge. "It's been awfully dull so far."

Larry and Pete were back at the press table in Special Sessions Court at 2:00 P.M., and they stood with the others while the judges entered. Then court was in session once more, and the next witness was ordered summoned. Assistant District Attorney Jacobson handed a slip of paper to the bailiff and he sang out in a loud voice:

"Judy Starr Hinemann!"

CHAPTER THIRTEEN

PETE MOREHOUSE got to the corridor very quickly and headed for the bank of telephones under the high windows. He saw Judy, dressed in a beautiful dark mink and a black felt hat and veil, entering the door held open for her by a tall, dark man, but he gave her only a glance. As a person, as a beautiful woman, she interested him not at all. As one of the vital pieces of this huge jigsaw puzzle that seemed to defy any reasonable solving, she was precious and important.

Pete dialed the *Press* and asked for Finley Browne. "This is Pete," he told the *Press* operator. "Give me his private wire."

"Yes?" said Browse.

"This is Morehouse. Judy Starr Hinemann has just been called as a witness for the State in the wiretapping trial of Wardell, Zannis and Balthazar."

"I'm damned. Where are you?"

"Just outside the courtroom."

"I was wondering where the hell you were... All right, God damn it, stay there. Cover it. I'll send Hymie. You see that Hymie gets a picture, or I'll have your hide."

"Will do," said Pete. He was grinning broadly as he hung up the phone and started back to the courtroom.

Judy Hinemann was just being sworn in. She stood relaxed, nonchalant, with her right hand raised and her left hand resting on the Bible. She had divested herself of her fur, and she was dressed in a plain black suit of exquisite cut and material that enhanced every line of her figure. There is no question about it that Judy, with her black suit and hat with its brief veil, made a beautiful widow.

Judy said, "I do," in her throaty voice, mounted the dais and sat in the witness chair. She didn't cross her legs; she tucked them back under the chair as far as they would go and sat on the edge, leaning forward and looking attentive. It was—the way she did it—an effective pose.

Pete sat down next to Larry Keene. Larry whispered to him, "This is going to be dynamite. Luke Wardell looks as though he were blowing a gasket. She hasn't looked at him once."

Martin Jacobson was on his feet, approaching the witness stand with quick steps. He asked Judy's name, age and address and then led her expertly through questions about her late husband and his business activities. When he had established all that he needed, he said, "Now Mrs. Hinemann, tell the court in your own words what you know about these three defendants, Luke Wardell, Morton Zannis and Louis Balthazar."

"I know they are employed by a company owned by my late husband, the Fifth Avenue Recording Company. Mr. Wardell is president and general manager, as well as attorney for the company. Mr. Hinemann told me that Mr. Wardell himself set up the company organization and hired all of the employees."

"Good. Now, Mrs. Hinemann, what is the business of this Fifth Avenue Recording Company?"

"Financial espionage through wiretapping."

Louis Balthazar was seized by a sudden fit of coughing, Luke Wardell poured him a glass of water from a pitcher on the table, and he spluttered water over the papers spread there. Then the coughing subsided and the questioning was resumed.

"Will you explain to the court, Mrs. Hinemann, just what you mean by this term, financial espionage through wiretapping?"

"Why yes," said Judy, smiling at Louis Balthazar, "it means stealing business and industrial secrets—you know, big stock market transactions—when some company would be trying to get control of a competitor; then you could find out what was happening to the price of the stock, and you could maybe buy in and steal it away from them, then sell it for twice as much. Another thing would be the information on a big campaign to sell some new product that would affect the price of the stock—or in reverse, when some product was a flop and the stock was due to take a tumble. There was a lot of that kind of information, and then there was the stuff you'd get from the bankers and the brokers, about rigging the market to send certain shares up or down, and about big loans that were going to be called, and about all sorts of people who were getting into trouble or who were making big killings."

"I see," said Jacobson. "Can you be more specific, Mrs. Hinemann? Can you give me an instance of how such information was used?"

"Well, one company is New Jersey Drug—that's NJD on the ticker. This New Jersey Drug was in real trouble about six months ago. They'd overextended themselves in a building program and then a couple of new products they had flopped, and they were right on the ragged edge. Luke Wardell found out about it through a tapped wire, and he began to sell their stock short—this was before there was a whisper of the trouble out in the market. So Mr. Wardell wound up owning the company. He owns it today, that is, the controlling stock in it."

"I see," said the prosecutor.

"Another one that Mr. Wardell owns is the Lackey Building. I bet not many people know *that*. Well, he got the Lackey Building right out from under the noses of the Weinstein Brothers when he got the secret dope on a mortgage they couldn't refinance. I can tell you all about that one. The mortgage was for $750,000, and the trouble was that the title wasn't clear. Something about the building line being almost a foot off, encroaching on the adjoining property. So Wardell got hold of this other property, and he forced the Weinsteins to sell to him for ten cents on the dollar. Henry Weinstein killed himself right after that."

"Am I to understand that Mr. Wardell used the information from this wiretap organization for his own profit, Mrs. Hinemann?"

Judy nodded vigorously. "Yes, sir."

"Who else used such information. Who else received it?"

"My late husband, Lamar Hinemann."

"How was this information conveyed to your husband, Mrs. Hinemann?"

"On recording tapes. Mr. Wardell would deliver the tapes to my husband several times a week at our home on Sutton Place. He would bring them in a briefcase and deliver them personally to Mr. Hinemann."

"You were present on such occasions?"

"Yes, many times. I knew all about the tapes and the wiretaps. My husband did not keep them secret from me. He told me all about the scheme and how it worked."

"Whose scheme was this, Mrs. Hinemann, this espionage?"

"Those three men," Judy replied, pointing. "Mr. Wardell, Mr. Zannis and Mr. Balthazar."

"How do you know that?"

"My husband told me, and he showed me the agreements drawn up for the Fifth Avenue Recording Company. I have those agreements."

"Do you mean to tell me, Mrs. Hinemann that your husband kept a record of this operation?"

"Yes, sir."

"And these are the records?" Jacobson picked up a packet of papers from his table and handed them to Judy. She examined them briefly.

"Yes, sir."

Jacobson had the papers marked for identification and introduced as evidence.

"What is in those records to connect these defendants with the wiretap operation in the Lackey Building?"

"Well, one is the agreement of what they are to do, what services they are to perform. Then there are their signatures. They all signed the agreement."

"What money changed hands at the time of the signing, Mrs. Hinemann?"

"My husband gave Mr. Wardell a check for $50,000. This was to be the retainer for his services for the first year of operation."

Pete got up and left the courtroom as quietly as possible, making his way to the telephones in the corridor. He got the *Press* city desk, gave a brief summary of Judy's testimony to Finley Browne, then gave a detailed account to George Houseman on rewrite. He had timed his call so that the story would make the last edition. When he had finished the call, he hunted for Hymie Lorentz, *Press* photographer. He found him in the clerk's office, talking to the busty secretary named Henrietta.

"Hello, Pete," said Hymie. "You got anything set up?"

"No," said Pete. "You grab her when she comes out of the courtroom, I'll run interference for you. She's with a big guy who looks very tough, so watch it."

"I'll get a picture," said Hymie. "No tough guy ever stopped me yet."

They went back to the courtroom door together, and Pete pointed out Judy to Hymie through the square of glass high up in the door. She was still on the witness stand, being questioned by Barron Eastman. Pete noticed half a dozen other photographers hanging around the corridor. He reentered the courtroom and resumed his chair at the press table. There were two more reporters there, a girl he recognized from the *News* and an old timer he knew very well, Jerry Finch from the *Tribune*.

He whispered to Larry Keene, "What's happened?"

Larry shook his head. "Nothing. She's making a monkey out of Barron, and *that's* something."

"...mean to tell me, Mrs. Hinemann that you did not profit personally in any way from this wiretap operation?" Eastman demanded.

Judy looked at him seriously and shook her head. "No, sir."

Eastman turned his back on her and moved leisurely to Luke Wardell's side at the counsel table. He bent his head and had a short whispered conference with Wardell. Then he straightened up and returned to the witness.

"How many shares of stock in the Lackey Building do you hold, Mrs. Hinemann?" he thundered at her.

There was no change of expression on Judy's face. She still had a serious, interested look.

"One hundred shares," said Judy.

"Ah... One hundred shares. And how did you get these hundred shares, Mrs. Hinemann?"

"Mr. Wardell gave them to me."

"And yet you knew, all of the time, as you have stated here under oath, how Mr. Wardell obtained control of the Lackey Building. Is that not a fact, Mrs. Hinemann?"

"No," she replied, her voice low, calm.

"Speak up, Mrs. Hinemann. What was your answer?"

"I said no," said Judy, smiling slightly. "I did not know at the time Mr. Wardell gave me the shares how he had got control of the building."

"Is it not a fact, Mrs. Hinemann that it was you yourself who called Mr. Wardell's attention to the information about the Lackey Building and the Weinstein Brothers on the recording tapes? That you obtained this information from the recording tapes yourself and passed it on to Mr. Wardell on the agreement that he would split with you on all profits? Is this not a fact, Mrs. Wardell?"

"No," said Judy. "It is not. That is a lie."

"It is a lie, eh? I wonder who is lying here, Mrs. Hinemann?" Barron Eastman stopped to mop his brow with his breast handkerchief. He shouldn't have. He should have kept talking.

Judy pointed a finger at him. "You are, Mr. Attorney," she said.

Judge Graham rapped for order. "We will have no more of that, Mrs. Hinemann," he said.

"I apologize," she said, turning to him. "Of course it isn't the attorney who lies. Not *this* attorney."

"That is all," said Barron Eastman. He returned to the counsel table and sagged into his seat next to Luke Wardell.

"No more questions," said Jacobson, rising. "You may step down, Mrs. Hinemann."

Judy came out of the witness chair and off the dais with a cat-like grace that many dancers acquire, and she walked through the wooden gate to her escort, who got up from his seat, holding her fur coat. She held her head high, and there was a slight smile on her lips as she passed the defendants' table. She didn't look at any of them. Wardell muttered something to her, probably a word that some men call women when they are angered, but she gave no sign that she heard it.

Pete got up and followed her, and when she and her escort reached the courtroom door he suddenly pushed past them and opened the door. He turned to them and said, "Oh, I beg your pardon. I'm in a terrible hurry." The man scowled at him, and Judy looked a little startled. Pete stepped quickly around the door, holding it for them, and just at that instant Hymie's flashbulb went off. They had been looking at Pete and they hadn't seen Hymie with his camera aimed.

The man glared and looked as though he were going to jump Hymie, but the little photographer turned quickly and started down the corridor. Judy said, "Never mind, Vince," and grabbed his arm. They started toward the elevators, holding newspapers up so their faces were covered, and Pete saw that the photographers from the other newspapers and press services were getting no good pictures. Hymie came back to him and said, "Who's the guy with her?"

"That's Vince," said Pete. "Probably Vincent DiCastro." He spelled the name as Hymie wrote it down on his caption card. "Fran Addams can identify him. Tell that to Browne."

Hymie left in a hurry to return to the office, and Pete went back into the courtroom. Martin Jacobson was announcing that the State had concluded its case against the three, and then Judge Graham ordered an adjournment until the next morning.

Pete and Larry Keene went into Judge Graham's chambers and waited until he was through conferring with Jacobson. Then Pete asked the judge if he had made an appointment for him with Gordon Buell.

"It's set for 5: 30 at Buell's office," said Graham.

Pete thanked him, and then Larry Keene said, "What do you think of this case now, judge?"

"I'll tell you one thing," replied Judge Graham, "that little girl has just succeeded in getting Luke Wardell disbarred."

Pete returned to the office with Larry Keene and went immediately to Finley Browne's desk and waited until the city editor was finished with a phone call. Browne hung up the receiver and grinned at the little librarian.

"That was good work, Pete," he said. "We scooped the town on that one." He snaked a final edition from a stack of papers on his desk and shoved it at Pete. The headlines read:

JUDY HINEMANN TELLS STORY
OF $1,000,000 WIRETAPPING

The story under it was topped with a line reading: *"By Pete Morehouse."*

"You could have made it ten million or a hundred million," said Pete. "You want me to do an overnight on it?"

"Sure enough. You got any new angles?"

"Yes. Wardell's not just going to sit and take his medicine. He's going to go down fighting. And these charges—"

"That figures. But that's up to the appellate division, and it's only incidental. Concentrate on Judy Hinemann. She's our story."

"O.K.," said Pete, "but now you're going to see all of this other stuff come out."

"What other stuff?"

"That ten-page memo I gave you, on all of these people."

Browne shook his head. "Look, Pete, one thing at a time. Now we're working on this wiretapping trial. Let's get that out of the way before we go for any balloon rides."

Pete said in a desperate voice, "Will you please listen to me, Finley? If you'll only let me work on this story—*really* work on it—I'll put that whole airliner sabotage right in your lap. I know what I'm talking about. Now they're all cracking up—they're beginning to fight among themselves and it's only a matter of time before they'll begin to talk too much."

Browne leaned far back in his chair and put his left foot up on his desk. He looked at Pete's earnest face and his blinking eyes and he scratched his head. "I've never known anybody so God damned tenacious as you," he said. "What the hell do you want, anyway?"

"I want to be a reporter again," said Pete simply.

"All right," said Finley Browne. "You're a reporter again. You go to work on it."

Pete stood there unable to speak. He was in a momentary state of shock. Then a smile spread slowly over his face. "You—you mean it?"

Browne nodded his shaggy head.

Pete said, "Thanks. I'll get to work." He wanted to say a lot more, but he didn't trust his voice. He turned abruptly from the city desk and went to a typewriter in the rear of the office.

Fran Addams watched him pass, unseeing, and she followed him and perched on the edge of his desk as he sat down.

"What gives?" she said. "You get a by-line on the lead story all of a sudden, and then you have a big row with Finley. What's going on around here?"

Pete looked up at her and swallowed. He cleared his throat. He lit a cigarette. "I'm a reporter again," he said.

"Whoopee," exclaimed Fran, disturbing the decorum of the entire editorial department.

CHAPTER FOURTEEN

PETE MOREHOUSE'S overnight on the wiretap trial and Judy Hinemann was, of its kind, a masterpiece. It was the first news story he had written in some ten years, and during that ten years of editing and criticizing the copy of others, he had learned a lot about writing. He had learned most of the secrets of readable presentation, of short and pithy sentences, of avoiding clichés and ungainly or complicated words, of stating facts unadorned with adjectives, to let them speak for themselves. His story was too long—much longer than stories usually ran in the *Press*—but it was so well done and so interesting that Sam Crowell, the night editor, wouldn't cut a line of it. He threw out a lot of other type and a picture to get it all in.

The story gave a complete run-down on Judy Starr Hinemann's background, from the Atlantic City high school and Arthur Winfield, through Angelo Scotti and Dutch Froelich right up to Lamar Hinemann and Luke Wardell and Vincent DiCastro. It was all there, Judy's life and her men, and written with such care that there could be no possible libel action.

Down in the middle of the story, in a reference to current the wiretapping trial and the backgrounds of the three defendants, there was one paragraph that had special meaning. Pete had spent fifteen minutes composing these hundred words, to make certain that they said just exactly what he wanted them to say, no more or no less. The paragraph read:

In connection with this trial, the spectre of Lamar Hinemann, the man who benefited by some $100,000,000 through this wiretapping, arises continually. Hinemann is dead; yet his spirit and his fortune live *on. The question arises...who killed Hinemann? Who placed a dynamite bomb in his baggage, if such was the case, so that he would die in the crash of the Paris airliner, along with the forty-seven other December travelers? Who was it that would seize thereby a large part of the millions stolen from the victims of this conspiracy? The answer to these questions will pale to insignificance today's sensation of Judy Hinemann's testimony.*

He showed his story first to Fran Addams, who had finished an overnight of her own. She read it carefully and then handed the copy back to Pete. She said, "That's a good story. I can see now how it is that you were able to teach me so well."

"Thanks," said Pete.

"But you as much as say that the Paris airliner was bombed so that Hinemann would die. Is that what you really think, Pete?"

He nodded. "Yes."

"You haven't very much to go on, have you?"

"Not evidence that would stand up in a court. It's something like that poisoning case over in France a few years ago, where the respected mother and farm wife wiped out her entire family and a few friends as well. All of these people around her began to die off, and the neighbors got to talking. Finally it became a certainty that she was poisoning them, but there was still no evidence that was any good in a court. They found poison in the bodies, but that didn't prove how it got there. They tried and she went free. Everybody knew but it couldn't be proved."

"I suppose this will have the same outcome."

"No," said Pete, "it won't. I'm working on it now—from now on. Pretty soon I'm going to have a lot of help. The difference about this, Fran, is that there's plenty of solid evidence lying all around, and as soon as the right people get interested, they'll find it."

Fran shook her head. "I don't see how you could possibly know that, Pete."

"Well, look at it this way: It wasn't a secret, one-man crime if I'm right and if Hinemann was the intended victim. Several people had to be in on it, and it's inevitable that they left clues around and that their actions can be traced. I don't know what the plot was, specifically, and what pattern will develop, but it's not going to remain in the category of that French poison case for long. Not after I get people stirred up."

Fran said, "I wish you luck."

"I'm having plenty of that. I'm a reporter again, and that's the big first step."

Pete was sitting in the anteroom of Gordon Buell's office at exactly 5:30. He had taken with him a copy of the ten-page memorandum he had written for Finley Browne, and he read this over, making corrections of typographical errors as he waited for the deputy police commissioner. Within five minutes he was in the commissioner's office, shaking Buell's hand and then sitting in the large leather chair at the side of his desk.

Buell was a handsome, white-haired man of sixty, who had spent his entire life in the police department, rising slowly through the ranks to his present eminence. His face was smooth and unlined, and he gave the deceptive impression of being a bland, mild person with little inward fire. Quite the opposite was true, for Buell was a fighter, primarily, and had been one of the toughest cops who had ever battled his way up through this toughest of all competition. Today in certain sections of the West Side his name was a legend, and his deeds were still talked about among those who admired or disparaged the law. It is a matter of record that Buell single-handed took three of the most dangerous members of the old Toohey gang into custody, delivering them on the verge of unconsciousness to the West 47th Street station in an ice wagon he had borrowed for the purpose. On this occasion he had walked into the precinct house without a mark on him except bleeding knuckles on his right hand and had announced that the depredations of the Tooheys was at an end and that he needed some help to bring in his prisoners because he'd had a sore back for several weeks now. And the sergeant had wondered later what Buell would have done to these men if his back had been well.

"Bob Graham tells me you have gathered some interesting information," he said to Pete. "You want to tell me about it?"

"I've got most of it written," said Pete, handing him the memorandum. "After you've read this, then I'll tell you what else I know."

The policeman took Pete's report and placed it on his desk in front of him. He read it slowly, puffing on a short cigar and rubbing the lobe of his left ear with nervous fingers. He didn't look up until he had finished. Then he leaned back in his chair and looked at Pete Morehouse.

"You a reporter on the *Press?*" he asked him.

"Yes," said Pete. "I've been assigned to this airplane story."

"You talked to Colby of the FBI?"

"No, but I will sooner or later. I've seen some of his reports so I know what the FBI is working on."

"We've been working on it, too," said Buell. "I've got four men assigned to this right now... You said you know something else, Mr. Morehouse."

"Well, yes. It's not so much what I know, it's what makes sense out of all this in view of what happened today in Judge Graham's court."

"Tell me."

"All of these things are tied together: Hinemann's death and Gower's death and Aganna's death and this chunk of money Mrs. Gower suddenly came into and, lastly, all of this wiretap and espionage conspiracy. Well, let's take one thing at a time. The wiretap. Luke Wardell blew the whistle on that himself. He's the one who tipped off the police and brought about the raid on the Lackey Building. He told that to Larry Keene, our financial editor, who is an old friend of his. He wasn't afraid to tell it to a newspaperman. In other words, he wasn't afraid who knew it. That's point number one.

"Mrs. Hinemann testified in court today that Luke Wardell got hold of New Jersey Drug and the Lackey Building through information he had received from the wiretap. That figures. She may have been lying like hell about everything else but not about that. It's too easy to verify. Well, it's so obvious that it escaped me altogether. But now that we know about it, this point number one begins to make sense.

"What I say is that Wardell wanted the wiretap all to himself, and the only way he could get the others out—Mrs. Hinemann and members of Lamar Hinemann's organization—was to dump it publicly and wreck it. Then when the trial was over and the shouting had died down, he would set up another wiretap. Because Wardell is the only one right now who has the know-how, that is, Wardell and his two boys, Zannis and Balthazar. Also, he's probably got all the equipment he needs stored away somewhere.

"Wardell has now found out, through Hinemann and his wife, who is no dope when it comes to big money, just how to make use of this wiretap information. How to swindle the swindlers, you might say. But the significant thing about all of this is that Wardell waited until Hinemann was dead before he moved. Why? I'll tell you why. It's because the wiretap was Hinemann's idea and was set up by Hinemann and was owned by Hinemann. Zannis and Balthazar worked for Hinemann and not Wardell. So Wardell couldn't steal anything while Hinemann was alive. With Hinemann dead, he could steal it all."

"That sounds reasonable enough," said Buell, throwing his cigar away and lighting a fresh one. "We can check on some of that, of course. We can also find out where and when the new wiretap is being set up."

"Another thing Wardell told Larry Keene," continued Pete, "was that he was going to marry Judy Hinemann. Well, Larry says this is completely out of character for Wardell. He's known Luke ever since they were kids together up on the West Side, and he says Luke is a misogynist and that he has a deep and active dislike for all women. Let's give him the benefit of the doubt and say that this Judy was the one exception. But even so, the fact remains that Judy will get all of the Hinemann dough and control of the Hinemann companies. So if Wardell was greedy enough to want to get the wiretap for himself, it follows that he would be greedy enough to want the rest of what Hinemann had—his wife *and* his millions. I'm just speculating, commissioner. But it all ties in, you'll have to concede that."

"It's a good case you make out," said Buell. "But didn't I read in your paper that Judy Hinemann testified against Luke Wardell?"

"That's right, she did, this afternoon. And that throws that fifty percent of Wardell's scheming right into the ashcan. He's lost Judy and he's lost the Hinemann dough. All he's got left is the wiretap."

"Double cross?" asked the Commissioner.

"That's what it looks like."

"Then your idea is that Wardell engineered this sabotage of the airliner to get rid of Hinemann?"

"That's one possibility. My idea is that Wardell got the dynamite bomb from this electronic genius who installed the wiretap, Willard Gower, and that he had it planted in Hinemann's luggage by the butler, Constantine Aganna. That would mean that Wardell had both Gower and Aganna killed and that he was the source of the $70,000 that Aganna gave to Mrs. Wardell to buy the restaurant in Atlantic City."

"We can check some of that easily enough," said Buell. "Wardell's bank accounts will show if there had been any large withdrawals around this time. Let's say about $80,000 at least. Aganna wouldn't have given it all to Mrs. Gower. We can find out what out-of-town hoodlums have been brought into the city, and if we're lucky, we may even find out who brought them in and for what purpose... You got anything else?"

"Yes. If it's not Wardell, then it's Hinemann's secretary, Vincent DiCastro, who planted the time bomb in his employer's luggage. DiCastro is the next most likely. The FBI's got a full report on him. He's been in Leavenworth and he has a bad military record. Also, he lives right next door to Judy, and he has a key to her apartment. If it's not DiCastro, then it's Judy herself, although she doesn't appeal to me as a suspect."

"There are more plots here than a B movie," growled Buell. "Let's take one at a time. We'll go to work on this Wardell angle. That sounds sufficiently good to me to warrant a little digging. By the way, what do you expect to get out of this?"

"A story," said Pete.

"A story, eh? Well, if we crack it, you may get your story. I can't protect you. We've got a lot of people in the department who talk to newspapers and who know what goes on. If you get beaten on your own story, I don't want you to come crying to me."

"I won't," said Pete. "That's the chance I've got to take."

"You want to work with any of my men?"

Pete thought for a moment. "Yes," he said. "I'd like to be around when they tear Gower's radio shop and his apartment apart."

"O.K.," said Buell, getting up and stretching his short, heavy legs. "Tomorrow morning at 8:00 o'clock be down at Nassau Street. Ask for Lieutenant Giles. I'll tell him you'll be there."

Detective Howard O'Malley of Brooklyn headquarters had an assignment he liked. Go to a bar and get drunk. Not too drunk, you understand, but drunk enough. What he didn't like about the assignment was the people he was to get drunk with—Danny Hamburger, a real crumb, and his bad news girl friend, Dora. Also it was away to hell-and-gone in Newark where he was to do this imbibing, and that took some more of the edge off it. Well, you couldn't have everything.

O'Malley rode the H. and M. tube to Newark and walked five blocks from the station to the Three-Star Bar and Grill. It was a blustery night with the thermometer not much above ten degrees, and he was glad to reach the warmth of the bar after the too-long walk. He banged the door shut behind him and came into a long, narrow room with a mahogany bar its entire length to the left and a row of wooden booths with tables and benches on the right. A jukebox to the right of the door was lit up and was blaring out a rock 'n' roll number in painful decibels. O'Malley took off his overcoat and put it over his arm, then started down the row of booths. At the fifth from the front, near the rear of the room, he came upon Danny and Dora sitting side by side, holding hands and arguing bitterly.

They stopped talking abruptly when O'Malley stood above them. Danny said, "Sit down, Howie."

O'Malley sat across from them, putting his overcoat on the bench next to the wall. "I'm buying," he said. "What'll you have?"

Dora said, "Listen to the big shot. He's buying." Then she reached a hand across the table and patted his cheek. "How are you, Howie?"

O'Malley nodded to her. "O.K. How's Dora-baby?"

Dora giggled. Danny said, "She's having one of her bad nights." The waiter came and stood by their table. "Dora and me are drinking bourbon and water."

"Make it three," said O'Malley. "Make it something drinkable like Old Forester."

"We got Old Forester," said the waiter, walking away.

Danny said, "What's it this time?"

O'Malley shrugged. "We're hunting for a couple of guys. It ain't important. I just gotta go through the motions."

"Yeah, I bet," said Danny.

"How's Zingy doing over here?"

"All right. He wants to get back home."

"To Brooklyn?"

"Yeah."

"He'll never. Not while four-eyes is mayor. Tell him he better buy hisself a house and settle down. Right here in Jersey."

"Who you hunting for?"

"Couple of hoods. They bump off two guys, one in Manhattan and the other right plumb on my beat in Brooklyn. I don't care about the Manhattan guy. They shouldn't of come over to Brooklyn. It makes me look bad."

"I bet. I'm crying for you."

"Give me a quarter," said Dora.

Danny reached in his pocket and put a coin on the table.

Dora put it in the record selector on the wall. "What you like?" she asked O'Malley.

"Anything but this rock 'n' roll."

"You're a square," said Dora. She started punching the buttons on the selector.

"Any strangers in town, Danny?" O'Malley asked.

"I thought you wasn't interested."

"Well, what the hell, I might as well know what's going on."

"Couple of guys from New Orleans."

"They come up to get away from the bad winter down there?"

"For a job. Joe Bird."

"Gunsels?"

"No, these guys are specialists. They don't leave no bodies lying around in vacant lots. They make it look like suicide."

"Joe Bird's a rat," said O'Malley.

"He's a rich rat. He's got it to burn."

"Big job, eh?"

"So they say."

"Where're these mugs?"

"Back in New Orleans. Augie and Louie they called themselves. Syndicate boys."

"Syndicate, eh? Where's Joe Bird fit in then?"

"Joe's got better connections than you think."

O'Malley sighed. "Life goes on. Things change. So now Joe Bird has connections…"

The waiter came over and O'Malley ordered another round. Then he said, "We want them two guys."

"O.K., go down to Orleans and get them," said Danny.

"I might just do that."

"In a pig's eye."

"Or I could let the G-boys do it for me."

"G-boys? Hey, you didn't say anything about that."

"Didn't I?"

"Goddamn you, O'Malley, if this is a federal rap, I'll cut your throat."

O'Malley laughed. "Just keep your lip buttoned, Danny, and you won't get in no trouble."

"No? How about Dora? She—"

"Leave me out of it," said Dora.

"She what?" asked O'Malley.

"Never mind," said Dora, "it ain't nothing to worry about. I'd just as soon see those two burn. I'd light the match." She laughed, a short, humorless sound. Then she drained her glass.

O'Malley looked at her a long time. Dora was the epitome of available sex. She was quite pretty and she dressed in a flashy way that showed herself off to any who would look. There weren't many guys down on this Newark level who wouldn't go for her. "You used to know a guy by the name of Bill Gower, didn't you?" O'Malley asked her.

Dora shrugged. "Can I have another?" she asked, holding out her glass.

O'Malley called the waiter and ordered three more, but doubles this time.

"I'm too sober," he said when the waiter had left.

Dora said, "I hear this Gower was killed in a subway accident."

"That's right," said O'Malley. He drained his glass.

"He used to come over to Newark when I was working for Lily," she said.

Danny said, "Why don't you keep your big mouth shut?"

"You wouldn't of known a guy by the name of Constantine Aganna too, would you?"

Dora shook her head. "Nope. Not by that name."

"You ever been to Gower's house?"

"In Brooklyn?" Dora asked.

"For Christ sake, *shut up*," said Danny.

"Oh, fiddle-de-de," said Dora. "Can I come over and sit by you, Howie? I'm getting tired of this crumb."

"I got to go after this drink," said O'Malley. "I got the duty at 8:00 A.M. tomorrow."

"You going to leave me, just like that, huh?" she said.

"You got your Danny," said O'Malley.

Danny looked at Dora with deep disgust. "I never seen a dame that didn't try to make trouble in a bar," he said.

O'Malley got up. "You two lovebirds stay here and fight it out," he said. "I got to get to bed."

"You sure as hell made up your mind in a hurry," said Danny. "You find out all you want to know?"

"Yeah," said O'Malley. "Thanks."

"Don't bother to come back no more," said Danny nastily. "I won't be here."

"You'll be here when I need you," said O'Malley grinning at him.

The anger left Danny's face as suddenly as it had arrived.

He nodded. "Yeah, I guess," he said.

CHAPTER FIFTEEN

LIEUTENANT MATT GILES was a peppery little grey man with bulging muscles on arms and legs and a skull full of information on a great number of subjects. His specialty was explosives and the maniacs who sought to use them to the peril of society. He was head of the bomb squad. He parked the black police sedan in front of 116½ Nassau Street at 8:00 A.M. Detective Harry Schaeffer, in the seat beside him, said, "Looks like he hasn't opened up yet."

Pete Morehouse, standing in front of the narrow shop window with the tarnished gold lettering across the top— ERHARDT & GOWER, Radio & Television Service-

Repairs—walked around to the driver's side of the sedan and introduced himself to Giles.

"I thought it would be you," said the lieutenant. "Get in back and we'll wait." He introduced Pete to Schaeffer.

"I saw you on television, lieutenant," Pete said.

Giles laughed. "I guess I'll never live that down."

"That was a tough question."

Giles shook his head. "I knew the answer—'a Man proposes but God disposes'—that was Thomas à Kempis. I got mike fright. Right at that crucial moment with $8,000 staring me in the face, I couldn't have told you my own name."

"Is that Erhardt?" asked Schaeffer.

They looked at a big man walking towards them from Park Row. He was dressed in a brown tweed overcoat with the collar turned up and a brown felt hat.

"That's him," said Pete.

They watched the man swing into the door of the small radio shop, take a keyring from his pocket and open up. He went inside, banging the door after him, and lights went on in the window. The three got out of the police car and followed Erhardt into the shop. Giles was in the lead.

Erhardt was in the back room when they came in. Pete looked around at the television sets piled almost to the ceiling. On the left was a small counter with a new cash register on top. Erhardt came through a door in the middle of the back wall and stopped, looking at the three. He had taken off his coat and hat, and he was dressed now in a maroon wool shirt and dark blue slacks. He recognized Pete immediately and scowled at him.

"You came back," he said.

Giles took a folded paper from his inside suit pocket and held it out to Erhardt as he walked to him. "I'm Lieutenant

Giles of the New York Police Department," he said. "This is a search warrant. Read it."

Erhardt took the paper and glared at the three. "Gestapo," he said. He glanced at the warrant briefly, then handed it back to the lieutenant. "Well, go ahead. Search."

The lieutenant and Schaeffer took off their overcoats and put them on the counter. Schaeffer went behind the counter and opened a large drawer under the cash register. Giles went into the back room, and Pete followed him. Erhardt stood near the doorway where he could watch both rooms.

The workshop of Erhardt and Gower was cluttered with radio and television chassis and parts, scattered on the floor and on the long workbench against the right wall. The bench had a score of drawers in it, and Giles went to the top drawer on the right-hand side, took the drawer out and dumped the contents on the top of the bench. Then he put the drawer back and started sorting out the dozens of small cardboard and metal boxes, pieces of wire and metal and other odds and ends, dropping them back into the drawer.

"They never throw anything away," he said over his shoulder to Pete. "This is going to be a long job."

Pete said, "I suppose you know what you're hunting for."

The lieutenant nodded. "Sure."

The telephone rang in the front room. Erhardt hurried to it, on the counter, and said, "Hello." He listened for a moment, then said, "Don't worry about it. I'll see you later." He repeated that several times at intervals. Then he hung up. He came into the back room and said angrily to Giles, "What do you mean by bothering my sister?"

"Who's your sister?" asked Giles mildly.

"You know who she is. Mildred Gower."

"Oh," said Giles.

"You've got men searching her apartment," accused Erhardt.

"Sure," said the lieutenant. "It's all legal. They have a search warrant, too."

"You're *worse* than the Gestapo," shouted Erhardt. "You can't do this! It's against the Constitution!"

Giles looked at him without expression. "You're making noises like a Communist," he said.

"I have my rights," exclaimed Erhardt. "I'm going to call my lawyer!"

"You do that," said Giles, turning back to his sorting.

Pete sat in a wood chair near the end of the bench and lit a cigarette. There was nothing he could do but wait. He heard Erhardt on the telephone, apparently talking to his lawyer. He seemed to be getting little satisfaction, by the sound of his voice.

Then Schaeffer came to Giles and showed him something. Pete got up and went to them to have a look. It was the silver case of an old-fashioned railroad watch. Just the case. Giles took a jeweler's magnifying glass out of his coat pocket and put it in his eye, then examined the inside of the back of the case.

"It's been in hock twice," he said. He handed the case back to Schaeffer. "When you're through in there, take it down and get a check on it. Find out whose numbers those are."

"I'm through now," said Schaeffer. "You want me to come back here?"

"No, I'll handle this. Get everything you can on that watchcase."

Schaeffer left and Pete went back to his chair. Giles said, "It's always amazed me how stupid people are when they set out to commit a crime. The simplest common sense would dictate that they get rid of all the evidence; that they leave no incriminating pieces lying around to connect them with the unlawful activity. But they never do. They always leave

143

fingerprints and tire tracks and pieces of wire and damning odds and ends. I've never known it to fail. All a cop has to do is to get a line on a likely suspect and then the evidence will turn up. It's always like that."

Pete said, "I take it you've got high hopes for that watchcase."

Giles nodded. "It would surprise me if it didn't connect up; it's just the kind of thing I'm talking about. Now look at this…" He came over to Pete with his palm outstretched. "This was one of the things I was hunting for."

Pete looked at the lieutenant's palm. There was a small, black object in it an inch and a quarter long. "Why, that's a watch hand," he exclaimed.

"Sure. A minute hand." He took a bit of tissue paper from his pocket and wrapped it up. "If you were making a timer for a bomb out of a watch, you wouldn't want the minute hand, so you'd take it off," he said. "What I can't get over is why, if you had an ounce of brains, you wouldn't throw it away?"

Pete followed the lieutenant back to the workbench and watched him sorting. "You expect to find something else?" he asked him.

"Maybe. Anything could turn up in these drawers, couple of sticks of dynamite or even a whole time bomb. Maybe they made a spare… Now here's something…." He picked up a small brass cap with two thin copper wires attached to it. "You ever see anything like that?"

"No," said Pete, "what is it?"

"This is a detonating cap put out by Hercules. It's got fulminate of mercury inside it. You attach one of these wires to the coil and the other to the switch on the timer. This is what sets off the charge of explosive. This, my friend, is the key to everything."

Pete thought that Giles was talking unnecessarily loud. He was certain Erhardt could hear everything he said. Just at that moment he heard the front door close. It closed softly, but the sound was unmistakable. He swung around the door into the front of the store. It was empty.

"Erhardt has skipped," he exclaimed.

"Sure," said the lieutenant. "I've been waiting for that. Ordinarily I don't talk so much or so loud, Mr. Morehouse."

"But he's got away," said Pete.

"No, he hasn't got away. If we're lucky, he'll take us to somebody else. Then we'll nail them both."

"Oh," said Pete.

Detective Howard O'Malley moved uncomfortably on the wooden bench under the single window in the squad room and yawned. His back ached and his mouth tasted like the sink in a Greek restaurant. He hadn't been to bed yet, and he had to fight to keep his eyes open. Detective George Farrell, his partner, looked up from his solitaire game with the greasy cards and said, "Why don't you go on home? I can handle it from here."

O'Malley shook his head and yawned again. "I'll wait," he said. "You want to take another look?"

"He ain't in yet."

"How do you know if you don't look?"

"I been listening. I could hear him."

"Go look," said O'Malley with a tired wave of his hand. "The only thing you can hear is the first call for lunch."

"Nuts," said Farrell. He started to deal another hand.

A plainclothes man came in, standing by the open door. His eyes were bright, and his face had an early-morning scrubbed look to it. "O'Malley?" he said. "The chief'll see you now."

O'Malley nodded to him and got slowly to his feet. He gave Farrell a disgusted look. "Come on, useless," he said, "let's get it over with."

They walked together down to the middle of the hall, following the plainclothes man, and went through a huge oaken door he held open for them. They were in a small anteroom with a desk and typewriter and a middle-aged woman with sleek grey hair and a freshly starched look on her face. "Go right in," said the plainclothes man, indicating a door through a pebbled glass partition.

O'Malley walked through the door, followed by Farrell. It was a huge office, larger than any down on Centre Street, even the commissioner's. There were two French windows in the far wall and across the corner to the right of them was a broad mahogany desk. Behind it was the chief, Steve Crandall. He stood up as they entered. He was as big as O'Malley, but he didn't look to be in as good shape. There was a noticeable bulge around his middle, and his shoulders had a white-collar slope to them.

"Always glad to welcome officers from New York," he said, shaking hands with them. "Have a seat, gentlemen."

"I'm O'Malley. This here is Farrell. We're strictly unofficial. I'm hunting for Joe Bird."

O'Malley sat in a leather chair facing the desk, and Farrell moved a wood chair next to him and slumped into it.

"Joe Bird," said Crandall. "Seems to me I've heard of him. Why would you come to Fort Hudson to hunt for him, Mr. O'Malley?"

O'Malley's face was expressionless. "Because he's been operating a floating crap game in Fort Hudson for the past two months," he said. Crandall glared at the New York detective out of icy-blue eyes. "Joe Bird is not in Fort Hudson," he said. "Hunt for him somewhere else."

O'Malley got up, and Farrell followed him to his feet.

"O.K., if you say so, chief," he said. "But I'll tell you something else. After we leave, then comes the FBI. You could save yourself a headache talking to us."

"So you say," said Crandall.

"So I say," echoed O'Malley. He turned and started for the door, Farrell following.

Crandall waited until he had his hand on the knob. "Come, back here, O'Malley," he said. "You, Farrell, go out into the hall."

O'Malley opened the door for Farrell, then closed it and returned to Crandall's desk. He sat in the leather chair again and took out a cigarette and lit it.

"We run a clean town here," said Crandall. "We don't get any bums and hoodlums, and we have no crime to speak of. Now and then an amateur gas station holdup or something of that sort, but no major crimes. No professional jobs at all. We—"

"Stow the lecture," said O'Malley. "I know the pitch. You play ball with the syndicate and they play ball with you. And what's a little gambling and other innocent pastimes, such as taking a needle of heroin now and then? Sure, you got a clean town. The hell with that. Where's Joe Bird?"

"Now see here," exclaimed Crandall, his face flushing with anger. "I'll have no more insolence—"

"Nuts," said O'Malley, getting up once more. "Look, chief, I've been up all night hunting for this hood. Either you give him to me or you don't. I'm too tired to argue. I don't want no lectures. I know all about Fort Hudson and you and the boys. I ain't interested. I just want Joe Bird."

Crandall picked a box of cigars out of a drawer and selected one. He bit off the end and spat into the cuspidor at the side of his desk. Then he lit it with slow deliberation. O'Malley stood looking at him, at his flabby face and blue jowls, and he wanted to lean across the desk and punch this face into a pulp. O'Malley didn't like people like Steve Crandall, and especially did he dislike them when he found them in a police department.

"Sit down," said Crandall. "There's no point in getting your back up. I'll see what I can do."

He picked up the phone on the side of his desk as O'Malley sank once more into the leather chair. "Give me George," he said into the phone. He waited a minute, then said, "George? There's a New York man here, O'Malley, Brooklyn headquarters. He's hunting for Joe Bird." There was another wait, then he said, "Find out from Eddie. Call me back." He looked up at O'Malley. "It won't take more than a couple of minutes," he said.

The telephone rang back almost immediately. The chief picked it up and placed his cigar in an ashtray. "Yeah?" He listened for several minutes, a look of incredulity spreading over his face. "The hell you say! Look, get somebody over to Eddie's right away. Clean it out. Get every Goddamned bit of equipment out of there fast. *Everything*, you hear? Stow it in Louie's garage. Now jump!" He banged the phone into the cradle and picked up his cigar, clamping it with his teeth. He glared at O'Malley for a moment; then his face relaxed and he leaned back in his chair.

"It's funny you should come hunting for Joe Bird this morning," he said. "You sure you ain't seen him? Last night down in Newark?"

O'Malley scowled at him. "Stop being cute," he said. "One thing I can't stand is a guy your size acting like a God damned pixie. What happened to Joe Bird?"

"If you were working for me. I'd beat that freshness out of you," exclaimed the chief, coming forward in his chair.

"If I was working for you," said O'Malley slowly, "I'd have you indicted in fifteen minutes. What happened to Joe Bird?"

Crandall looked at his cigar, rolling it in his fingers. It was a fight, getting control of his temper. Then he said in a reasonable voice, "They found Joe Bird in Newark Bay. They think he was shot. Two boys saw his body in the mud at low tide and reported it. They think he was dumped in last night, or maybe the night before. Not any longer ago than that. They'll know after the autopsy. What did you want him for, O'Malley?"

O'Malley got to his feet and stretched his legs. He tried to fight back a yawn, but it won, and he put a hand over his mouth. "We were hunting for him for a couple of murders," said O'Malley. "Well, be seeing you. Thanks for the hospitality, chief, and a Merry Christmas."

He walked out the door into the anteroom and nodded to the starched face. "You better get your boss a box of aspirin," he said. Then he went out into the hall and found Farrell pacing nervously. Farrell came up to him quickly. "How'd you make out," he asked.

O'Malley shrugged. "Not so good. Joe Bird is dead now in Newark. We go down there, George, and look at the body."

"You got any ideas?" asked Farrell as they headed for the front door of the building.

"No," said O'Malley. "Just curious."

CHAPTER SIXTEEN

AFTER TWO HOURS with Matt Giles at the radio shop, Pete went to Special Sessions to cover the end of the trial of Wardell, Zannis and Balthazar. The end came at 11:30 when Presiding Judge Graham intoned, "We find the defendants Luke Wardell, Morton Zannis and Louis Balthazar guilty as charged. The prisoners are remanded in custody for sentencing on Monday, December 30."

Pete phoned in the story to the *Press*, then went uptown to have luncheon with Fran Addams and Cameron Hawkes in an Italian restaurant on 57th Street. They talked mostly about him—about his being a reporter again and the story he was working on.

Hawkes told him once more, "I wish the hell we could forget that lost airplane."

Pete said, "That story's just started. You're going to see a million words written about that crash before we're through with it."

"Maybe," said Hawkes. "It depends on whether they find out who did it."

"How about the FBI?" asked Pete. "They getting anywhere with young Faulkner?"

"Not that I hear of. Harrington told me today they're still questioning him."

"It's a waste of time. It won't be Faulkner."

"Who will it be, Pete?" asked Fran.

"It might be Luke Wardell," said Pete. "It might be, and then again it might not be."

"Wardell?" exclaimed Hawkes. "You're completely nuts."

Pete shook his head. "No. Maybe fifty percent nuts but not completely."

When he returned to the *Press* office he found a message from Gordon Buell. The deputy commissioner wanted Pete to call him after 10:00 P.M.

Pete told Finley Browne of the message. "It looks like I'll be working late," he said. "I think maybe Buell is going to give me a story."

"What story?" asked Browne.

"About the airliner sabotage," replied Pete. "I think things are beginning to move—that Buell has made an arrest."

"Hey," exclaimed Browne, "that's something. You call me if it's anything hot."

"Sure," said Pete.

It was lacking a few minutes of midnight on Christmas Eve when Pete Morehouse climbed the stairs at Centre Street to the office of First Deputy Police Commissioner Gordon Buell. He had been on the go since 6:00 P.M., when he had risen from his bed in Floral Park, but he felt as fresh as the northerly breeze that was sweeping the city clean of the day's accumulation of fumes. He felt exhilarated; he felt reborn—that life was beginning all over again for him. That is what being a reporter once more did for Pete.

He knocked on the door of the deputy commissioner's office, then opened it and saw that the anteroom was empty. He walked in and opened an inner door. Buell and another man were huddled at the corner of the mahogany desk. The commissioner looked up. "Come in, Pete," he said. "I've got someone here I want you to meet."

The visitor got up as Pete approached. He was a big, hard-faced man in his late thirties, his thick black hair neatly combed and a look on his jowls of having been freshly shaved.

"This is Howard O'Malley of Brooklyn headquarters—Pete Morehouse of the *Press,*" said Buell. "O'Malley has been tracking down some people for us."

Pete shook hands with the detective. They both sat, Pete in a chair at the center of the desk. Buell said, "Continue, O'Malley. Mr. Morehouse is in on this."

O'Malley gave Pete a dubious look, then said, "I get it that this Joe Bird had got himself in with the syndicate. How they took him in I'll never know. He was a little ratty guy with no guts, a whiner. Back in forty-forty-one he was over in the docks for awhile with Crespi, and he got to be sort of assistant secretary. Then when the syndicate took over and dumped Crespi in the river, the best he could do was to roll drunks.

"We got him for that in forty-two and sent him away for a year. He showed up again in New York right after the war, and for two years he worked for Morton Zannis. You see how all these people keep tying in, commissioner? Gower and this Constantine Aganna and Joe Bird and the mugs from New Orleans and the syndicate... I took a look at Joe Bird over in the Newark morgue, and it was a clean job, through the side of the head with a small caliber gun, no bigger than a .32. There were powder burns, so he didn't have no place to run. There were no other marks on him.

"I'd say it was done in an automobile. I got the Newark boys to hunt for the car—but you know how they are over in that borough. They'll never find it. That was a good tip, commissioner. Where'd you get it?"

The commissioner waved a hand at Pete. "This reporter dreamed it all up. He found the connection between Gower and Aganna."

O'Malley looked at Pete with new interest. "Is that a fact? Say, this is the first time I know a newspaper guy to do anything but obstruct."

Pete grinned at him. "We're not like that," he said mildly. "We try to get our stories, sure. That's our job. Intelligent cops cooperate with us."

"That could be a dirty crack," said O'Malley.

"Nothing personal," said Pete. "I take it you've found out who killed Gower and Aganna?"

O'Malley nodded. "That we did."

Buell said, "O'Malley has some very good connections in New Jersey. That's where we found it. This Joe Bird he was talking about brought two men up from New Orleans. They are the syndicate specialists in the more subtle forms of homicide—what the boys call the quiet bump. They make it look like accident or suicide, and they're expert enough that they get away with it more often than we'll ever know. They got Willard Gower in the subway and Constantine Aganna on the ship.

"The Aganna case looked very sloppy at first. The two men had waited for him until he came aboard and then had left him shot through the head. There was the suicide note of course, but that looked at a first glance to be too ridiculous to bother with. An obvious phony. Well, you know something, Pete? That note was in Aganna's handwriting believe it or not. We've had it checked by the two top experts in that field, and they both swear to it.

"That leaves us with no case there, regardless of what we know. We just have no evidence. Same thing with Gower. Sure, the two men were seen with him on the station platform form by the motorman. He said that they seemed to be trying to hold him and that Gower appeared to break away just as the train entered the station and leaped down onto the tracks. That's what it looked like to him. You figure out how they did it; I can't. Another thing I can't figure is why Joe Bird was shot and dumped in the bay. That makes very little sense to me."

O'Malley said, "I've been wondering a lot about that commissioner. I keep asking myself, why would the syndicate bump off one of its own hoods after he had arranged for Gower and Aganna? Well, there's one way it adds up. Suppose Joe Bird was working on his own for somebody else and used the two syndicate disposers from New Orleans only because he knew where to get them? So then the syndicates doesn't like this caper at all, and they get rid of Joe Bird. It would add up that way, but I got to admit it leaves a lot of questions without answers."

Buell nodded. He took a cigar box from his desk drawer and offered it to Pete, who declined, and then to O'Malley.

"Christmas cigars," he said. He selected a cigar for himself and bit off the end, then lit it with a desk lighter. "The major question is," he said, puffing to get the cigar started, "why would the syndicate object? If we can find out that, then we'll know why Bird was bumped and a whole lot more about all of this."

"I'll ask around," said O'Malley. "That dumb Steve Crandall over in Palisades could tell me, but if I go back there with a question like that, the chances are I'll wind up with a busted head."

Pete said, "I can make one guess that's not too far fetched. Let's assume that Joe Bird was hired to do this job by Wardell. Wardell is a good bet because of the Zannis tie-up; also he has defended any number of hoodlums, and maybe Bird was one of them. The records would show that. So Joe Bird took on the commitment without clearing with his bosses. Well, there was a guy on that airliner by the name of Aldo Vincenzi. I don't have to tell you who he is. So the bosses got mad because Vincenzi is dead, and they eliminated Joe Bird."

"That's a long way around the block," said O'Malley. "You got too many *if*'s in that, and besides, Vincenzi is dead anyway and bumping Joe Bird, is not going to help him any, or even revenge him... Who's this Wardell you talk about?"

"Luke Wardell, the attorney," said Buell. "Pete here thinks Wardell is the tie-up with Gower and Aganna and the sabotage of the Oceanic airliner on December 5. You remember that?"

O'Malley scratched his head. "Brother! Is that what we're working on?"

"That's what we're working on," said the commissioner.

"In that case," said O'Malley, "why not keep it simple? Whoever hired Joe Bird for this job had him bumped off so he couldn't identify 'em. It doesn't matter whether it's a syndicate killing or not."

"You want to go back over to Fort Hudson with that question?" asked Buell.

"Sure," said O'Malley, getting up. "The pitch is, it's not a syndicate job. That's what we think, but we've got to be certain. Will this louse Steve Crandall please tell me, so we don't have to be mad at the organization hoodlums?"

"He'll say no in either case, won't he?" asked Pete.

O'Malley shook his head. "No. If it wasn't the syndicate he'll tell me so. That'll be honest. If it was, then he'll have me thrown out of Fort Hudson on my ear. There's one thing you can always depend on about the boys. If it's a bum rap they'll cry like babies about how innocent they are. If it's not, they just get mad... Well, good night, all."

The commissioner waited until O'Malley had closed door, then he said, "We're making progress, Pete. Today we arrested two persons."

The commissioner sat back in his chair and puffed on his cigar, Pete waited a moment for him to continue. When he didn't, Pete asked, "For the sabotage of the airliner?"

Buell shook his head. "No, not quite. There is no charge yet. No, these are the people who are involved in the manufacture of the time bomb that was put aboard the airliner."

"Erhardt," exclaimed Pete. "Erhardt and who else?"

"His Sister, Mildred Gower."

Pete said, "I was with Matt Giles when he searched Erhardt's shop this morning. There's not very much evidence, is there? I mean, there's nothing you could take into a court?"

Buell straightened up in his chair. "No. The evidence doesn't mean much unless we can connect it up. Matt found a watchcase and a minute hand and a detonator in Erhardt's shop. Walter Casey found four sticks of dynamite in Mildred Gower's apartment. That was after Erhardt had phoned her from a drugstore near Borough Hall and told her to sneak out on the pretext of going shopping and meet him at the Atlantic Avenue Station of the L.I.R.R. So when they met, he asked her if the cops had found 'it' yet and she said no. That's when we picked them up... The dynamite was in a hole in the wall in the kitchen covered over with some new wallpaper. And that watchcase—that checked out to be an Illinois railroad watch bought by a man who could have been Willard Gower down on the Bowery on November 16.

"That's our evidence. We can prove, with it, that Erhardt and his sister had knowledge of the manufacture of a time bomb made from the parts of a watch and charged with dynamite of such and such a trade name purchased on November 9 last at Doylestown, Pennsylvania, by a man who will probably check out as Kurt Erhardt himself.

"I've been in this business for nearly forty years, Pete, and this is the first time I've ever taken a reporter into my confidence while I'm working on a case. Newspaper reporters have always been poison to me; they nearly cost me my job with all that drivel they wrote about me in the Toohey case some years back. Well, now I've got an idea. I've got an idea that maybe I can use a newspaper reporter. How do you feel about being used?"

"That would depend," said Pete. "You tell me what your idea is."

Buell remained silent for a moment, puffing on his cigar and tapping his desk with a pencil. "We can't toss this Luke Wardell into a cell and scare him into talking. We can't even pick him up and question him with any hope of learning anything. He's an attorney and a pretty high-class guy. He's not going to scare and he's not going to sit in a cell jittering; he'd get himself out within an hour. And he knows more about questions and answers than anyone in the department. We've got him linked to Erhardt and his sister through Gower, and we've got him linked to Hinemann and Mrs. Hinemann and Morton Zannis. Also, we've got Mrs. Hinemann double-crossing him in this wiretap case, which would indicate that there's more there than meets the eye. Now then, there's the butler, Constantine Aganna, and that dough he gave Mrs. Gower to buy the restaurant in Atlantic City. There's no doubt in my mind at all that that money could have come from Wardell. We've been looking into his bank accounts all day, two of them that we know about. There's been a turnover of more than $100,000 in those two accounts since the last week in November. More than half of this sum was drawn out in cash... That's the situation with Wardell.

"I've been sitting here for sixteen hours asking myself; how can we get to him? What can we do to put the pressures on him and force him to make some mistakes? I'll tell you this, Pete that's the only way we're ever going to get him. Make him trip over his own feet. Well, we've got two aces, Erhardt and his sister. We've got them locked up, and we can keep them for a couple of days, but we're going to have to charge them with something if we keep them longer. So, we've got to move fast if we're going to use them at all. That's where you come in. You write the kind of a story we need, and it may blow this whole thing wide open."

"What kind of a story do you need?" asked Pete.

"One that says Kurt Erhardt and his sister have been arrested in connection with the sabotage of the Oceanic airliner. The story has got to be very clear about that; it has to say that we have found out who made the bomb that destroyed the plane and that other arrests are to follow. Also, there has to be plenty in it that would indicate to a smart reader that Erhardt and his sister are talking and telling all they know."

Pete said, "That would be a hell of a story if it was true."

"It's true enough," said Buell. "You don't have to let your conscience bother you about that. And anything that doesn't pan out we'll take the blame for. Why I've given you all of the background is so you'd be willing to go along with us and not say too much. The story's got to be vague about some of the details. We just can't say exactly what we have and what we haven't. You get the point?"

"I think I do," said Pete. "It's not the kind of thing a newspaper would do, ordinarily. What I mean to say is, we publish all of the news we can get, and we don't allow any censorship—not by anybody."

Buell shook his head. "You want to solve this airliner sabotage, don't you?"

"Sure. That's the whole point."

"This is the way to do it, then. It's the only way I can figure out to make the maximum use of what we've got."

"All right, I'll try it," said Pete. "But we don't publish tomorrow, Christmas Day. I'll have to run it Thursday. You want to see the story I write before I turn it in?"

"Read it to me," said the commissioner. "I'll give you my private number at home."

CHAPTER SEVENTEEN

PETE MOREHOUSE'S first story on the investigation of the time bombing of Flight 900 of Oceanic Airlines appeared in the first edition of the *Press* on the day after Christmas, Thursday, December 26. The story appeared under his by-line, occupying the last two columns on page one. Two eight-column headlines read:

2 HELD IN AIRLINER SABOTAGE;
POLICE FIND TIME-BOMB CLUES

The story jumped to page two, running for two more columns. Much of it was a rehash of the tragedy and of the sabotage investigation by the FBI. Revealed for the first time was that the New York Police Department had been conducting an investigation of its own. The wallop of the story was in the first half dozen paragraphs. These read:

New York detectives, working under the direction of Deputy Police Commissioner Gordon Buell, have made their first arrests in their independent investigation of the time bombing of the New York-Paris airliner that carried Greta Fortune to her death along with forty-seven others, it was learned exclusively today by the New York Press.

Held without bail in connection with this mass murder are Kurt Erhardt, 42 years old, proprietor of a radio repair shop at 1160 Nassau Street, and his sister, Mrs. Mildred Gower, 37 years old, of 1537 Sterling Place, Brooklyn. Mrs. Gower's husband was killed on December 6, the day after the airliner was blown up, under a subway train at Chambers Street. He was the partner of Erhardt in the radio repair shop.

Commissioner Buell said last night that his detectives and members of the bomb squad under Lieutenant Matt Giles have found evidence that the time bomb that destroyed the luxury airliner was manufactured in the radio repair shop of Erhardt and Gower and in the Gower apartment.

"We have found indisputable evidence that the timing device and the detonator for this bomb were assembled in the radio shop," the commissioner stated. "The bomb in its final form—probably that of a Christmas package—was put together in the Gower apartment."

The Commissioner declined to elaborate upon the evidence. "I can say no more about it or about the two suspects at this time," he said. "However, you can quote me as saying there will be further arrests shortly. The mass murder of these air travelers is not completely solved, but we are now over the first hurdles. Other culprits are known and will be in our hands very soon."

Commissioner Buell told this reporter that this was the first break in the sabotage of the Oceanic Airways luxury flight that took to their deaths, besides Greta Fortune, her husband Mark Cassell, producer-writer; Aristotle Coulardis, shipping magnate; Lamar Hinemann, financier and reputed to be one of the wealthiest men in the world; and a host of others prominent in the financial and social life of two continents.

The commissioner declared that there have been three other murders in connection with the sabotage and that the full story of these as well will be revealed in due course.

That was all that was new in the story, but it was considered to be sufficient. Pete had read it to the commissioner, who had asked for no changes; then he had called Finley Browne at his home. The city editor had obviously been celebrating Christmas Eve with drinking companions, and he was in no mood to discuss business. He stopped Pete after the first paragraph and said, "Leave it for Sam Crowell. He'll handle it. I'll see you Thursday morning."

Pete then had gone home to Floral Park, arriving at 3:20 A.M. He woke up Cissie and gave to her the Christmas present he had bought for her with almost all of his savings— a golden ballet dancer set with small rubies in the form of a pin, which she had admired once in an expensive jewelry store.

He was in the office at 8:00 A.M. Thursday, and Finley Browne called him to the desk before he had a chance to take off his coat and hat. Browne was holding proofs of the story in his hands, and he was scowling darkly.

"What the hell is this, Pete?" he demanded. "Who are you trying to kid?"

"I'm not trying to kid anyone."

"Sit down. Let's have a talk." Pete sat and Browne continued. "What are these two people charged with, this Erhardt and his sister?"

"They haven't been charged yet," said Pete.

"Oh, they haven't been charged yet, eh? Then how could they be held without bail?"

"The commissioner asked me to put that in. He wanted to give the impression that—"

"Who the hell is running this newspaper?" interrupted Browne. "Gordon Buell? All right, let's skip that, for the moment. You say, '...have found evidence that the time bomb, which destroyed the luxury airliner, was manufactured in the radio repair shop of Erhardt and Gower and in the Gower apartment. That's just dandy. Unidentified man found dead on beach. Spoke French fluently. How do you know? How could anyone possibly know? What possible evidence could be found that would prove the time bomb, which destroyed that particular airliner, was manufactured anywhere by anyone? You get my point, Mr. Morehouse?"

Pete nodded. He had known these things, of course. He said, "The other day you told me I was a reporter again and that I was assigned to this story. Now Gordon Buell and a half a dozen detectives are working on the angles I dug up. I'm not a cop, I'm a reporter; so I had to get the police to do the police work. Buell and his men are on the track of something hot, and if we run this story, it will help them. That's all."

Finley Browne sighed and leaned back in his chair. "You'd make this newspaper look silly, you'd make us look like a bunch of stumbling amateurs just to help the police?"

"No," said Pete, "it's not for that. It's for the story, so that when it does break I'll get it."

"Suppose I don't run this story? I've still got time to yank it out."

"I can't do anything about that," said Pete. "I'll resign, of course. I wouldn't be any more use to you or the *Press* then."

Browne looked at him and scowled. "It's the God damnedest thing I ever heard of," he said. "Using a newspaper for—for what? Blackmail? Coercion? We don't work that way, Pete."

Pete nodded. "I know, Finley. I'm wrong as hell. But if we run this story as is—with all the absurdities in it—then we'll have the airliner saboteurs right in our laps. I thought it was worth it."

"Maybe it is," said Browne, looking at the proofs once more. "You know, it's not a bad story. And the average reader would never catch on… God damn it, why don't you let me in on these things?"

"I called you at your home—"

"On Christmas Eve!"

Pete said, "You've known me for a long time, Finley."

"Yeah. Faith. That's what I need, faith."

"It's a good time of the year for it," said Pete.

"All right," said Browne. "But if you're wrong, it's going to be your neck and not mine. I'll kick you on your bardot right out of the newspaper business."

Pete got up. "Fair enough," he said.

The headlines sold 80,000 extra papers on the day after Christmas—an unheard of circulation gain for that day.

At 10:00 A.M. Pete was called to the office of the publisher, Colonel Wilson Gaylord. He found Gaylord and the general manager, William Barr Polk, drinking coffee that had been brought down from the lunchroom. Pete was told to take a seat facing them, and the publisher asked him if he wanted coffee. Pete thanked him and said no.

Gaylord said, "Finley Browne tells me you are a reporter again, Pete. Congratulations."

"Thanks."

Polk said, "That's a very dangerous story you wrote for our paper today, Mr. Morehouse."

"In what way is it dangerous, Mr. Polk?" asked Pete.

"There is a million-dollar libel suit in it," said Polk, his face flushing angrily. "I am surprised that Mr. Browne and Mr. Victory had so little judgment as to let it get by."

"Shouldn't you talk to them about it, then?" asked Pete. "I wrote it, sure. But I have no authority about what goes into the paper."

Gaylord said, "We have talked to them, Pete. They both told us that you could explain why the story was written and why it should run... I don't share Mr. Polk's apprehensions about a libel suit. Our laws in New York are a little more liberal than those of Kansas and Missouri. However, now that the question has been brought up, I should like to know the inside of this."

"Libel is libel, whether it's New York or Kansas," said Polk. "I have been informed on very good authority, there are not even any charges against these two people who were arrested and that the police will be forced to release them today, or tomorrow at the latest, with apologies."

Pete looked at the little general manager and fought against showing his dislike. Here was a Napoleon who was going to make life miserable for all around him because had not grown as tall as he thought he should be. Out in Kansas City, Pete had heard, they had nicknamed him "Heart-Disease Polk" because of the great number of persons who had succumbed to his nastiness. Pete said, "would you please tell me, Mr. Polk, who is this good authority who warned you against libel?""

"Certainly not."

"I was wondering," said Pete, "because the story comes from Gordon Buell, first deputy police commissioner, and it was written at his request in exactly its present form so that Mr. Buell and his detectives could solve a vicious mass murder, and that of the sabotage of the Oceanic airliner."

"That is not what I hear," said Polk. "I am told that the story is the opening gun in a campaign of lies and vilification against certain persons who are in no way connected with the sabotage of the airliner. What do you think of that?"

"Very little," said Pete. "It sounds as though someone with a guilty conscience were trying to make a sucker out of you, Mr. Polk."

The general manager spluttered, and Colonel Gaylord stepped into the breach. "Will you tell us the background of this story, Pete?" he asked.

Pete then gave a complete account of his meeting with Buell and of the various occurrences that had preceded it. He left out only one name, that of Luke Wardell. Pete had heard when Polk had first come to the *Press* that he had been a friend of Wardell and that they were often in each other's company.

When he had finished, the publisher said, "I see no harm in cooperating with the police in this way *if*, as you say, we shall benefit by it with an exclusive story of the sabotage. In fact, I am all for it."

Polk continued to disagree. "It is too dangerous for me," he said. "I wash my hands of it. When the libel suit comes, please remember that I warned you."

Pete said, "The only person in town who would take a case like this is Luke Wardell, and he's going to be disbarred in a day or so, so we don't have to worry about him."

Polk became really angry then. He said, "Wardell is a gentleman, and you are obviously not, Mr. Morehouse."

Colonel Gaylord said, "You run along, Pete. I'll fight this out."

Pete went back down to the editorial department and phoned Gordon Buell. The police operator switched him to the commissioner's home, and he heard a sleepy voice answer the ring.

"Buell talking."

"Sorry to bother you, commissioner. This is Pete Morehouse. I had no idea I'd be waking you up."

"Time I got up, anyway. Been in this bed for a couple of hours. What's on your mind?"

"I was wondering if there'd been any reactions yet."

"Probably. I've been out of touch. I'll be in my office at noon. You want to come over?"

"I'll be there. Somebody called our general manager, Polk. Told him the story was libelous. Said something about a campaign of vilification against innocent persons…"

"Is that so? Very interesting."

"Wardell is a friend of Polk."

"Well, well. See you at noon, Pete."

At 11:30 P.M. Barron Eastman appeared before Judge Harry Donnovan in County Court, Brooklyn, seeking a writ of habeas corpus on the persons of Kurt Erhardt and Mildred Gower. Within five minutes the Kings County district attorney, Fred Kilgallen, was in court opposing the writ. The bombshell he dropped was this: "Erhardt and Mildred Gower are at this moment on their way to homicide court, Manhattan, to be arraigned on a charge of accessory to the murders of forty-eight persons, and so it is respectfully requested that this writ be denied."

"Writ denied," ruled Judge Donnovan.

At 12:00 o'clock Pete walked up the stairs at police headquarters and into the office of Gordon Buell. Right behind him came Calvin Colby of the FBI. Buell introduced the special agent to the newspaperman, and then the two sat in leather chairs at the side of the commissioner's desk.

Buell said, "Morehouse is the man who gave us our, original information." He took Pete's report from the top drawer of his desk and handed it to the FBI man. "This is the report I told you about. I consider it of great value."

Colby started reading, and the commissioner lit a cigar. Pete said to him in a low voice, "I heard Erhardt and Mrs. Gower were being arraigned, just as I left the office."

"It's just a technicality to hold them," said Buell. "The murders, if any, weren't committed in the county, so we won't gain much by it except a little time."

They waited for Colby to finish. He handed the report back to the commissioner and turned to Pete. "From what, I understand, some of this has been substantiated. I like the evidence that was obtained at the radio shop and at Mrs. Gower's home. That will be invaluable to us. Mr. Buell says you have a further theory of this crime, Mr. Morehouse."

Pete told him about Luke Wardell in detail. It was much the same story he had told to the commissioner.

"Wardell is a possibility," Colby conceded.

"I've been thinking a lot about the others, too," said Pete. "I think a good prospect is Vincent DiCastro. The more I think about him, the better he appears to me. There's his background. It's just as good, if not better, for this sort of crime as that of young Faulkner."

Colby looked surprised. "What do you know about Faulkner?"

"I knew you were investigating him, that's all. We—we have various sources of information. Well, DiCastro was in the apartment and he helped pack Hinemann's bags. As Hinemann's secretary, he would be tied up with Luke Wardell and the wiretap. He would be tied in with Zannis and Balthazar, and through them with Willard Gower. He was working with Constantine Aganna in that household, and through Aganna he was tied in with the Gowers and with Erhardt. He was a lot closer to that setup in many ways than Wardell... The trouble with Wardell is the question of access to Hinemann's bags. The only way he could have gotten a package into one of them was to have Aganna do it, or possibly Mrs. Hinemann, and that's not so very likely. What kind of story could he have given them? If it was Mrs. Hinemann, of course, you'd expect that by this time she would have come forward and told it. She now seems to dislike Wardell. Look at her testimony against him at the wiretap trial—I suppose you know about that? So let's assume that if he did plant the bomb, it wasn't through her. But Aganna would be even more unlikely. Somehow or other, the idea that Wardell would try to buy Aganna for $70,000 or $80,000 doesn't add up. It seemed to at first, but couldn't Aganna have gotten twice that from Hinemann for double-crossing Wardell? Aganna didn't owe Wardell anything that we know of, and I think Wardell is too intelligent to have taken such a chance. There's got to be more than money... So here's DiCastro in the same household, and probably very close to the butler. He would see him every day, and Aganna would work for him just as much as he did for the Hinemanns, maybe even more so. Maybe then it was DiCastro who gave Aganna the money and then had him killed to keep him quiet."

Colby nodded. "DiCastro is a better suspect in many ways than Wardell," he said. "There's one thing wrong with DiCastro at this time, however, Mr. Morehouse. That's motive. Wardell had the motive and not a very good opportunity; DiCastro had the opportunity and no motive that we know of. A man doesn't kill his boss, the goose that lays the golden eggs, just to steal his wife."

"You know about DiCastro and Mrs. Hinemann?" asked Pete.

"We have been questioning DiCastro," said Colby, "ever since Commissioner Buell told us of his interest in this aspect of the case."

"I didn't know that," said Pete. "Have you been questioning Wardell, too?"

Colby shook his head. "No. We may, but as you have pointed out, he had no opportunity. We cannot place him at the Hinemann apartment on December 5."

Pete said, "I wonder why Wardell got so upset at today's story in the *Press*, then?"

"Did he?" asked Colby.

Pete told the FBI man of his meeting in the publisher's office. "I don't know that it was Wardell, but I don't know who else it could be, either."

Colby thought about it for a moment. "It could be that Wardell knows a lot about this—that he fears a direction the inquiry may take and is trying to head it off… Well, I feel that we may be on the track of something that may prove productive. The Bureau is highly appreciative of your efforts, Mr. Morehouse."

Pete said, "What I am interested in is the story—when it breaks. I'm a newspaperman only. I have no other concern."

"I can't protect you on that," said Colby coldly. "But I will inform Commissioner Buell of any action we may take long before the newspapers are told. What the commissioner does with the information is his own business." Then he smiled at Pete.

"Thanks," said Pete.

CHAPTER EIGHTEEN

ON THURSDAY AFTERNOON Pete went to Larry Keene's office behind the low wooden railing at the very rear of the editorial department and perched on the edge of Larry's desk.

"We've got things stirred up now," he said. "I figure that with any breaks, we'll have the full story of the airliner sabotage wrapped up in a few days."

"Yeah?" said Larry. "Who done it?"

Pete shrugged. "I don't know yet. It's a race between Luke Wardell and Vincent DiCastro."

"Wardell?" exclaimed Larry. "My God, man, are you sure?"

"No," said Pete. "Nobody's sure. That's why I wanted to see you. How about you fixing it for me to talk to Wardell?"

Larry leaned back in his chair and looked at Pete. "What do you think, boy? That he'll drop right into your lap like a ripe plum, with confession all typed and signed?"

"No, not at all. The fact is, I'm betting it wasn't Wardell. You know him, Larry. He'd see you and he'd talk to you. Maybe you could fix it up and come along with me and we could find out something."

"Like what?"

Pete shrugged. "I don't know. There are more angles to this thing than a skinny dame in a bathtub. I just can't leave it alone, I guess. I can't wait. What I want to ask Wardell is about him and Judy Hinemann, but I don't suppose he'd talk about that... Would he, do you think?"

"He might," said Larry, "after Judy's double-cross at the wiretap trial... All right, I'll phone him and see what he says. When do you want to see him?"

"Right now."

Larry picked up a private phone on a table beside his desk and dialed a number. He said, "Luke? This is Larry Keene. I'm sorry about your troubles, boy. I guess I didn't help to make them any easier for you...No, that's all right. It's a job...Sure, but I won't. That isn't why I called. Guy here by the name of Pete Morehouse wants to see you...Yeah, he's the one. He works here too, just as I do...I'd come up with him if you'd see him...No, I won't let him...O.K., in about half an hour?...So long, Luke."

He hung up the phone and nodded at Pete. "He'll see us right away, as soon as we can get up there."

"What won't you let me do?" asked Pete.

"Write the interview with him and run it in the paper."

"Oh," said Pete. "I didn't want to do that, anyway."

"That's what I thought," said Larry.

The two went down the elevator and got a cab in front of the building. They talked shop on the way uptown, Larry complaining about lack of space and the policies of Browne and Victory that kept his stories off page one. Pete's beef was about his expense account. He had just had his first one trimmed a third that morning.

Larry paid for the cab, and Pete followed him to the door of Luke Wardell's house. The frozen-faced butler answered their ring and took them to the library on the second floor after taking their overcoats and hats. Wardell shook hands with Larry, then with Pete as Larry introduced him. He was in a dressing gown and slippers, and he needed a shave. His eyes were blood-shot, and there was a deep tiredness about his face and in his movements. He mixed a bourbon for Larry, poured a glass of sherry for Pete, then sat in a chair facing the coffee table where a bottle of Scotch reposed and poured himself a straight drink in a four-ounce glass. Pete and Larry sat on the divan facing him.

Wardell said, "I know you are not here to dance at my funeral, but that's the way I feel. I feel that way about everyone right now. It'll take another week or so for me to come out of it… What do you want to know, Larry?"

"Pete's the one with the questions," replied Larry.

"Shoot," said Wardell, looking briefly at Pete, then down at his glass.

Pete asked, "Why did Judy Hinemann testify against you at the wiretap trial, Mr. Wardell?"

Luke shrugged tiredly and sipped his Scotch. "That's a woman's prerogative, to act like a woman. I suppose she changed her mind about me. Maybe she's found someone else who will do her dirty work."

"Someone named Vincent DiCastro?" asked Pete.

Wardell nodded.

"You did her dirty work?" said Pete.

"Some of it. I did what she wanted, for a long time. I suppose I would have done anything for Judy."

"Do you want to be specific, Mr. Wardell?"

"No." He shook his head. "That's all done with, water down the sewer. That's what I'm sitting here forgetting with this bottle. Well, I made out all right, when you add it all up. I wasn't cheated out of a thing."

"You did plan to marry her?" Pete asked.

"I don't know. That's what I thought for a time, but now I don't know. If you want the truth, I probably would have run like hell at the last moment."

"Maybe she knew that."

"Maybe. Probably."

"Did you read my story in today's *Press*, Mr. Wardell?"

He nodded.

"What do you think of it?"

"It wasn't much. I think Gordon Buell is away out on a limb and that he's going to have to retract everything he said. But that's his business."

"You think it was libelous?"

"Yes," he said. "Erhardt and his sister can sue your ears off as soon as those ridiculous charges are dropped."

"Why do you say the charges are ridiculous?"

"I'll ask you a question," said Wardell. "How could anyone ever prove that the Gowers and Erhardt had knowledge of the particular time bomb on that particular plane, to say nothing of having made it?"

"By a confession," said Pete.

"There isn't any confession," scoffed Wardell.

"No," said Pete, "but there will be."

Wardell shook his head. "Not unless those people are insane. If they don't confess, they're safe for the rest of their lives."

"I wonder," said Pete. "The history of such crimes is the confession. It seems to be inevitable; you always find it."

Wardell didn't say anything. He poured more Scotch into his glass.

"You know a guy named Joe Bird?" asked Pete.

Wardell didn't hesitate or act surprised. "Yes," he said. "The late Joe Bird."

"Have you seen him lately?"

"Not for a couple of years. I defended him twice, once on a mugging charge and the second time on gambling. Then he moved out of New York for good."

"You know where he moved to?"

"Jersey. Last I heard he was doing well in Fort Hudson with the syndicate. He was a sad sort of little man, a nothing. The syndicate must be hard up for help to have taken him on."

"You didn't have him bumped off?"

Wardell laughed, a short bark with little humor in it. "No."

"How about DiCastro? Did he know Joe Bird?"

"Probably. He used to spend a lot of time at Joe's dice games at Fort Hudson, I understand."

"Is that a fact," exclaimed Pete. "Who told you that, Mr. Wardell?"

Wardell closed his eyes and rubbed a nervous hand over his unshaven face. "I know about him. DiCastro is quite a gambler. He'll bet on anything. I suppose the biggest bet of his life was that Lamar Hinemann would die on that airplane."

"You want to explain that?" asked Pete.

"I have good reason to believe that DiCastro was dipping his fingers into the till. Mr. Hinemann told me late in November that his auditor was worried over a matter of $138,000 that seemed to have vanished. He said the auditor was making a final check and that if the figures refused to balance out, he wanted me to see the district attorney."

"Did he mention DiCastro?"

"No...that's just my guess."

"Who is Hinemann's auditor?"

"Davidson-Falk. On Madison Avenue."

Pete took a folded packet of copy paper from his pocket and a pencil and wrote down the name, then put them away.

"You've got something more to go on than a guess, haven't you?" Pete asked.

"I'm pretty tired," said Wardell, suddenly slumping in his chair. "Do you mind if we call this off?"

Larry got up. "No, Luke. We'll go."

Pete said, "Thanks very much, Mr. Wardell." He followed Larry to the door, and they both turned and looked at the attorney. His eyes were closed, and he seemed to be sleeping, Larry shook his head and said, "The poor bastard."

The butler helped them with their coats and let them out. Pete said, "I'm taking a cab downtown. You want me to drop you?"

"At Grand Central," said Larry. "I'm going home."

On the way downtown Larry said, "He's sure as hell in a mess."

"He's a funny guy," said Pete. "He talks like an honest man; yet everything he's done says he isn't."

"Luke has too much personality," said Larry. "That's been his downfall. He can charm anybody. The whole world rolls over for him, waiting to be taken and loving it. Next year he'll be back on top again, restored to the bar and hypnotizing juries. But tonight he's got his troubles... What do you think now about the airliner sabotage?"

"Hell, I don't know," said Pete. "I'm not a detective. I'd say Wardell had nothing to do with it—that it was DiCastro if it was anybody, but I'd probably be wrong. It'll turn out to be Wardell sure enough, or the butler, or somebody's uncle from Australia. Or even Judy Hinemann."

"I thought you were the bright boy who was feeding all of the information to the police," said Larry. "Finney Browne told me you got this whole Hinemann angle stirred up."

"Sure, I did that. But it was all there, all of the facts, I just arranged them so they made sense in a particular way...I'm not trying to solve any crimes, Larry, I'm just trying to develop a story for the paper."

The cab stopped at Grand Central and let Larry out, then continued on down to the *Press* office. Pete went up in the elevator to an empty editorial room. It was 6:00 P.M. and the night staff wouldn't be coming on for several hours. He sat at his desk and looked out the window, then rolled a sheet of copy paper into his typewriter and began to write an account of his interview with Wardell. He wanted to get it down on paper so that he could look at it and see if it revealed anything. He didn't think it did. He didn't think Wardell had told him anything that he would ever be able to use in his story, the Big Story that he would be writing very soon now.

The telephone rang. Pete answered and heard Cissie's voice. "There is a Mrs. Morehouse calling a Mr. Morehouse. Is there such a person as Mr. Morehouse?"

Pete said, "Hello, Cissie."

"Are you coming home?" she asked. "Ever?"

"Sure, honey. I'll be along in a little while, I've got a couple of things to do. I'm waiting for a call."

"Why don't you come out to Floral Park and wait for it?"

"That's a hell of an idea. I may just do that."

"Listen, Pete, aren't you carrying things a little too far? Sure, it's wonderful to be a reporter again. There's nobody happier about it than I am—for you. For me, it's worse than being a widow. If you were dead, now, I could get used to it sooner or later, I could adjust myself to not seeing you any more. But when you're still alive and I don't see you it's—it's upsetting."

"You know I'd die for you, any time."

"That's not funny. Are you coming home or aren't you?"

"In a little while, honey. I've got something here to finish. I'll try to catch that eight o'clock train."

"You be on it," said Cissie. "If you're not, I'm walking out."

"Going home to mother?"

"I should say not! I hate Ohio. I'll go down to New York and have myself a ball. I'll move into a hotel and live it up. I'll get away from this dreary house."

"We can't afford anything like that," said Pete, alarmed.

"That's your problem. I'm just not going to stay here alone another night."

"I'll be on the eight o'clock," said Pete. "Keep some stew warm. I'm going to be hungry, too."

"All right," said Cissie. "That sounds better."

Pete finished the Wardell interview, folded it up and put it in his pocket, then picked up the phone. Mabel Garth said, "Hello, honey. You going home?"

"You were listening!" exclaimed Pete.

"Sure. It's awfully lonesome around here this time of the evening. Say, if I was Cissie, I would walk out. You're a rat, Pete Morehouse."

"For God's sake, are all you dames in a conspiracy? Well, I'm leaving right now. Any calls come for me, put 'em out home."

"You expecting Gordon Buell to call, honey?"

"You know too much."

Pete left the building and took the subway to Pennsylvania Station. He slept all the way to Floral Park. The conductor, Jake Krantz, an old friend, woke him up just before the train came to a stop. Cissie was waiting for him at the station in the Ford.

"You were pretty sure I'd be on that train, weren't you?" he asked her.

"I've got an overnight bag in the back," she said. "If you weren't, I was going to drive into New York."

"You actually meant that, then?"

Cissie laughed. "Well, I was going to invite you over to my hotel. I couldn't have any fun there alone."

When they drew up in the driveway beside their box-like house, they heard the telephone ringing. Cissie said, *"Oh, no."*

Pete hurried in through the kitchen door and picked up the phone. It was the police operator from Centre Street. "Just a moment," he said. "Commissioner Buell has been trying to reach you."

Pete waited and Cissie came in. She went to the stove and turned the fire up under a large pot. Then she filled the coffeepot with water and put that on. Buell's voice suddenly came over the wire.

"Pete? We've got it!"

"You've got it?"

"Yep. It's DiCastro."

"I'll be damned."

"We're questioning him now. Colby will take him off our hands in an hour or so and book him."

"He's confessed, eh?"

"No," said Buell. "He hasn't."

"I don't get it," said Pete.

"Judy Hinemann bailed us out," said the commissioner. "She's been with us since five o'clock. She gave us the motive. She's got him practically strapped into the chair. You coming in?"

"Yes, of course. Is it my story?"

"All yours, Pete. There hasn't been a whisper."

"I'll be right in. Thanks, commissioner."

"Oh, you're welcome, my boy."

Pete hung up the phone and turned to look at Cissie. Her back was to him as she stood over the stove.

"This is the story," said Pete. "They've arrested Vincent DiCastro for sabotaging that airliner."

Cissie turned and beamed at him. "I knew you'd do it!" she exclaimed.

"I—I didn't do anything. I get the story, that's all."

"I know. We'll eat, then I'll drive you in."

"That'll take too long."

"It's all ready, Pete. You've got to eat something."

"You're not angry?"

"Because my husband is the best reporter in New York? Don't be silly."

"It'll be all night again," he said. He picked up the telephone and put in a call to Finley Browne. Cissie put two heaping plates of stew on the table and sat down opposite him. They began to eat while Pete waited for his call to go through.

Then he got the city editor and told him briefly of the arrest of DiCastro and Judy Hinemann's part in it.

"That's terrific," said Browne. "Can we keep it exclusive?"

"I think so," said Pete. "That was my agreement with Buell, in so far as he would be able to."

"All right. You cover Buell. You get that story and write it. I'll get somebody over to see Mrs. Hinemann right away."

"Better send Fran Addams," said Pete. "Judy knows her well now, and she might talk to her."

"Great. Do you think she'll stand for a photographer?"

"She might," said Pete. "It's worth a try."

"I'll be in the office," said Browne. "I'll see you after you've talked to Buell."

CHAPTER NINETEEN

WHEN PETE MOREHOUSE got to Gordon Buell's office, he found the deputy commissioner sitting on the edge of the desk in the anteroom talking to two detectives. He was chewing on a stub of cigar and his short white hair stood on end around his head, giving him the appearance of a chrysanthemum. He waved a hand at Pete and said to the detectives, "Go through that place carefully and don't miss anything. If you find them, call me back here."

The two left and Buell shook hands with Pete. "Looks like we've done it," he said. "You ready to go to work?"

"Any time," said Pete.

Buell motioned with his thumb to his inner office. "We're still working on DiCastro," he said.

"Is he doing any talking?"

Buell shook his head. "Nothing. He will say absolutely nothing. He wants to see his lawyer."

Pete took a thick fold of copy paper and a pencil out of his pocket and sat behind the desk. "Start from the beginning, commissioner," he said.

"Mrs. Hinemann phoned me about 4:30 and said she wanted to see me—that she had some vital information," said Buell, chewing on his cigar. "I told her to come down. She arrived about five, alone. She had on a year's pay in furs and a little black hat with a veil on it. Widow. A hard-faced, blonde widow. She told me she had read your story in the *Press* and she'd been thinking about it ever since. It worried her, she said, because she knew something about somebody that fitted in with every detail of that story. It scared her, too, she said, and she wanted to know if we would protect her.

"I reassured her about that, and then she said that this person had been very close to the butler, Aganna, for a reason that had puzzled her up to then. She said that she had inadvertently seen a check he had made out in Aganna's name for $85,000, drawn on his own bank account. She said she didn't know whether he had actually given the check to the butler, but she supposed the bank records would show that.

"Then I asked her to stop being coy and tell me whom she was talking about. She said I didn't have to be so impolite about it and she was talking about Vincent DiCastro, her late husband's confidential secretary. I questioned her about this check, and her story seems to stand up, so far as I can determine. Then I asked her what else.

"She said DiCastro had been acting in a very unexpected way towards her ever since December 5. She said that he had a key to her apartment, of course, and that he had been coming in at odd hours and making a real pitch, asking her to run away with him to Europe and saying that he loved her and wanted to marry her. What was strange about it, she said, was that before December 5 their relationship had been no more that of employer and employee and that he had been careful to keep his place. He had never, by word or act, indicated any personal feeling for her, nor had he sought to be friendly, she said. In fact, he had ignored her.

"I asked her a lot of questions about that, too, and her story seems O.K. There were too many details and specific instances for her to have concocted it...I'll admit, Pete, that I was pretty skeptical at first. She didn't make a good impression on me when she came into my office, and I was ready to discount everything she said. The more I listened to her, the more convinced I became that she was sincere, that she was telling me the truth. Tomorrow we'll see how some of these details check out—the $85,000 to Aganna, for instance—but right now I'll accept most of what she said.

"I told her that this information might become very important but that it didn't really prove anything yet. I asked her to tell me exactly what she had in mind about DiCastro.

"'Don't you know?' she demanded.

"'You tell me,'" I said.

"She didn't say anything for awhile—just sat there looking at me and thinking things over. Then she said, 'I think DiCastro put the bomb on that airplane to kill my husband. DiCastro and Aganna packed his bags and it would have been the simplest thing in the world for DiCastro to have put a time bomb in his baggage.'

"I told her I agreed with her—about the opportunity. I told her that we were very much interested in DiCastro for that reason, but that up to now we had been able to find no possible motive for his having done so.

"Her eyes lit up, then, like a couple of automobile headlights in a fog—you know, not bright, but you knew the light was there. She said, 'I can tell you that, commissioner. I was saving that for last.'

"This is what she told me: Point A—DiCastro was more than $100,000 short in his brokerage accounts that he kept for Mr. Hinemann. The auditors had discovered it and were ready with a full report on it upon her husband's return. Point B—It was Vincent DiCastro into whose keeping had been placed the 40,000 bearer bonds of Texas Exploration, of which there was no record of ownership. She said these bonds actually were hers, a point she said DiCastro did not know. She said that these bonds he planned to keep for himself. They are worth, she said, some $4,750,000 at the current market.

"The matter of the shortage already has checked. We called Hinemann's accountants and they verified it. The bonds we are now hunting for. Mrs. Hinemann says they were in a safe deposit box downtown that DiCastro had access to but that she has reason to believe DiCastro removed them from this box on December 5 or 6 and has since secreted them somewhere, probably in his own apartment. If they're there, we'll find them.

"I guess that's about it. You got it all, Pete?"

Pete nodded. "I've got it. It's a hell of a story, commissioner."

"It is that. With Judy Hinemann's testimony, we'll get a conviction without any trouble... Now there are a few other details I haven't given you. I'll tell them to you, but we want them kept quiet for the present. We're still not through with this investigation, you know. One is that Mrs. Hinemann told me, in response to a question that DiCastro knew Joe Bird and had been to Bird's gambling layout many times. Another is that DiCastro knew both Willard Gower and Kurt Erhardt and that he had got Erhardt and Gower to install all televisions and radios in the Sutton Place penthouses."

"All you've got to do is to prove that DiCastro hired Joe Bird to kill Gower and Aganna, then killed Bird," said Pete.

The commissioner shook his head. "No, we won't have to prove that. DiCastro will give the FBI a complete confession as soon as they start showing him the evidence we've collected."

"There are two points that I can tell you about," said Pete. "I was talking to Luke Wardell earlier, and he told me about the shortage in DiCastro's accounts. He said it amounted to $138,000."

"That's the figure I have," said Buell. "What's the other point?"

"That DiCastro did know Joe Bird. Wardell also says DiCastro spent a lot of time in Fort Hudson at Bird's establishment."

"That's fine," said the commissioner. "I'll get Wardell in here."

"Can I have a look at DiCastro?" asked Pete.

"Sure." The commissioner got up and opened the door to the inner office. Pete followed him in and saw Hinemann's secretary sitting in a wood chair facing Buell's desk. Two detectives were sitting on the edge of the desk side by side talking to him. Off to the right at a small portable table was a police stenographer tapping the keys of a stenotype machine.

Vincent DiCastro looked like a man who was seeing the end of his life. He was a man resigned to oblivion. His shoulders sagged; his head bent forward as though he was waiting for the blow of the executioner's axe. There was no life in his eyes, which shifted continuously, never resting anywhere for more than a brief instant. His mouth sagged loosely, and the hand that took the cigarette from his wet lips shook with nervousness.

"No I didn't," he was saying, his voice low and strained. "No I didn't. I took nothing that was not mine. I refuse to answer any more. I want a lawyer."

Pete stood for a moment at the edge of the commissioner's desk watching him. He wanted to tell people in his story what DiCastro looked like, how he seemed to be reacting to his arrest.

"We'll find those bonds soon enough," said one of the detectives. "You took them. We'll prove that."

The other detective asked him, "Who did you hire to knock off Joe Bird? Or did you do it yourself?"

DiCastro glanced briefly at each, looked at Pete for a moment, then lowered his eyes to his cigarette.

"I didn't kill anybody," he said with great weariness. "I want an attorney. I have a right to have an attorney."

The door opened, and Calvin Colby came in with two other men. He was dressed immaculately in a blue cashmere overcoat and holding a crisp grey hat in his hand, in sharp contrast to all of the others in the room, who looked disheveled and tired, even Pete Morehouse.

Colby shook hands with the commissioner and with Pete. Then he looked hard at DiCastro. He moved to his side and put a hand on his shoulder. He spoke to him, his voice quiet, "All right, old man, come with me."

DiCastro got slowly from his chair. He didn't look at the FBI man. He buttoned the collar of his shirt and slipped his tie into place. "O.K.," he said. "Where to?"

Cissie Morehouse went with her husband to the editorial room on the second floor of the *Press* building on Park Place. She had bought a couple of paperback detective stories at a drugstore while she had waited for Pete at headquarters, and she sat at the empty reception desk in the entry hall and arranged the desk light so that she could read comfortably.

"Take as long as you have to," she said. "I'll wait here."

Pete went into the city room and saw Finley Browne at his desk talking on the telephone. Two photographers were sitting on the bench where the office boys rested between errands, and Pinky Vincent was going through a huge stack of telegraph copy. Over at the managing editor's desk, Phil Rausch, picture editor, was showing a picture layout to Sam Crowell, the night editor. The rest of the staff had not come in yet. Pete sat in the chair beside Browne's desk and waited. When Browne hung up the phone, he said:

"DiCastro's gone for good, now. The FBI's got him."

"Fine," said Browne. "Anybody else at headquarters know about this?"

"None of the reporters."

Browne leaned back in his chair and put his foot up on the desk. He grinned at Pete. "This is what I like," he said. "It's all ours. God! I bet we pick up more than 100,000 on this story. I was just talking to Harry Markey in circulation. He said if it holds up for a couple of editions tomorrow, he'll buy you a new hat."

Pete then pulled the notes from his pocket and gave Browne a full account of the story—everything Gordon Buell had said and everything he had observed in Buell's office.

Browne listened intently. When Pete had finished, he asked, "How about this angle on Gower, Aganna and Joe Bird? How safe are we calling Gower and Aganna murders?"

"It's safe," said Pete. "We just can't say yet who killed them. Probably it was DiCastro who hired the job done. Same with Joe Bird. However, it all belongs in the story."

"Give it just a passing mention," said Browne. "I'll have a side story done on that with all the details. I've got George Houseman coming in at 1:00 A.M., and I'll turn it over to him. George can really write a story like that."

"Anything else?" asked Pete.

"Yeah. Fran Addams is up talking to Judy Hinemann now. She's got Les Howard with her, and she phoned in a while ago to tell me Judy was posing for pictures. I'm going to try to talk Sam into running an eight-column layout of her right across the top of page one. She's one hell. of a looking dame."

"I'll leave Judy to Fran, then," said Pete. "You want any more side stories?"

"What did you have in mind?"

"We ought to do one on Gordon Buell. He was the one who had the imagination to see something in all of this. If it wasn't for Buell, there would be no story about Kurt Erhardt and his sister, and there would have been no talking by Judy Hinemann. It was that story that did it."

"You say that in your story," said Browne. "Take all the credit you can yourself, too. Sure, we'll do a piece on Buell. Good idea."

Pete went back to his desk and started to write. He wrote steadily for three hours, so completely absorbed in his task that he was unaware of the city room around him. He didn't see the rest of the night staff come in, or any of those of the day staff who had been called in for this special story. He didn't even see Fran Addams, who had taken her place two desks to his left and was writing her own story. At 2:30 A.M. he put "—30—" at the bottom of the eighth page of copy, pulled the sheet from his typewriter and lit a cigarette.

He looked around and he saw Fran. She was bent forward at her typewriter, her face serious, concentrating on each word that she tapped out. Pete wanted to talk to her, but he decided against interrupting. He went back to his own copy and started to read through it, editing it ruthlessly as though it were a story by someone he disliked, a rather inept reporter who seldom used the right words to express himself.

He took his copy to Finley Browne and handed it to him, Browne started to read it, and Pete walked out to the foyer. He sat on the edge of Cissie's desk. She looked up at him and smiled. "All through, Pete?"

"For tonight," he said. "Let's go back to Floral Park. Tomorrow, maybe, I'll get a chance to write the real story."

"What do you mean by that?" Cissie asked as she got to her feet.

Pete shrugged. "I just don't like this story about Vincent DiCastro. The more I think about it, the less I like it. I keep seeing the way DiCastro looked in Buell's office—a dead man. There's something about it that isn't right. I can't tell you what it is."

Cissie said, "You're tired, Pete. You'll feel differently about it in the morning."

"No," said Pete stubbornly. "I won't."

CHAPTER TWENTY

PETE MOREHOUSE'S story of the arrest of Vincent DiCastro for the mass murder of the forty-eight persons aboard Flight 900 to Paris on December 5 shook New York as few stories ever have. It was comparable in public interest and reaction to the exclusive *New York Times* story on the kidnapping of the Lindbergh baby, or Kennedy's exclusive Associated Press story announcing the end of the war in Europe. The presses could not turn out the papers fast enough, nor could the trucks deliver them in sufficient quantity to satisfy the public demand. Everywhere you looked in the city on this Friday morning—on the streets, in the subways, in offices and stores and in hallways—you would see the double eight-column headlines in the *Press:*

HINEMANN'S SECRETARY
HELD AS PLANE BOMBER

The circulation figures soared, and the entire *Press* building, from the coffee shop on the top floor to the rumbling pressroom two stories underground, echoed to the accomplishment in the single word across the top of the first page: *EXCLUSIVE*. It was that word that meant everything precious in the dubious profession of newspaper reporting and in the seldom rewarding activities of the editorial department. When you could put *Exclusive* across the top of your first page and then follow it up with such a story as this, you had paid them all back with interest, all the people who counted the money and bewailed the expenses—the business manager and the stock holders and the advertising managers and the publisher. That made you even.

But the story did not stay exclusive for long, of course. Within two hours all of the city's afternoon papers had headlines to outdo those of the *Press* and pictures of Judy Hinemann on their first pages. But the *Press* had done it first, and everyone knew that the *Press* had done it first. The head start gave them an edge that they never relinquished, and at the end of the day the circulation figures, based upon the press run, showed a total that was 250,000 above the normal Friday's figure.

Not much of New York knew that this was Pete Morehouse's story. Everyone, of course, saw his name on the top of the last two columns on the first page, but the name meant nothing to them, and they didn't remember it seconds after reading it. What they remembered was the story itself and the spread of pictures across the top of page one, just under the headlines of the beauteous Judy Hinemann.

The other by-line on page one that was not remembered was that of Fran Addams, but her story, like Pete's, was read by everyone and enjoyed even more than Pete's factual news account. Fran's story was about a fascinating personality, and there was the light touch about her writing of the expert woman reporter, a touch never achieved by any man. Fran wrote of Judy as though she were the girl next door—the girl you saw every day on her way to the store or hurrying to catch a train downtown—and she came remarkably to life. You got to know her very well in this column and a half of type, and you sympathized with her and you shared her problems and her apprehensions and her hesitation in revealing this awful thing she had found out about a member of her husband's household.

The trouble with the story was that it was about a woman who was kind and warm and chaste, a woman who didn't exist. This Judy Hinemann didn't gibe in any way particular to the Judy Hinemann Pete had got to know through Fran Addams, in the courtroom at the trial of Wardell and his associates, and through the newspaper clippings in the *Press* morgue.

Pete bought a first edition of the *Press* from blind Joe Royle and started to read Fran's story as he waited for the 9:33 into the city. He had had only four hours of sleep, and his eyes smarted and his mouth tasted dry; but his mind was keyed up even sharper than it had been the other days of this week, and he was impatient to get back to the office and back to work on the story. He read through Fran's interview quickly, hunting for some realistic and revealing paragraph, but he didn't find it. Then the train came in, and when he got aboard and settled into a seat in the second car, he started to read the story again, much more slowly and carefully.

When he got to the office, he learned that Fran was out on an assignment. He left word with the operator that he wanted to talk to her when she called in.

He telephoned Gordon Buell. The commissioner was in a cheerful frame of mind, and he complimented Pete. "I've got some more for you for tomorrow," he said. "I'd rather give it to you here. I don't like this telephoning much."

"I understand," said Pete. "I'll be right over."

Pete told Finley Browne that Buell had some new developments and that he was going to his office.

Browne said, "Sure. You handle it. You assign yourself, Pete. I give it all to you."

When Pete got to Buell's office, the commissioner told him that his men had found the missing bonds of Texas Exploration and that the case against DiCastro, so far as he was concerned, was just about completed.

Pete asked, "Where were the bonds found, exactly?"

"They were sewn into his mattress. That is, all but 1,000 of them. The bundle was exactly 1,000 bonds short. Now here's another thing. DiCastro had arranged to move out of that apartment. He had called a moving company and he had arranged for all of his furniture to be stored. It was to have been picked up today and carted off to a warehouse. That is how he planned to hide his loot."

Pete was making notes, and after he finished he said, "That's a funny place to hide anything like that. Why didn't he get himself another safe deposit box and put them there?"

"I don't know," said the commissioner, spreading his hands. "Who can tell why people like that do anything?"

"Did you find a sewing kit in his apartment?"

"A what?"

"A needle and thread. He'd have to have that to sew up his mattress, wouldn't he?"

"Sure. I suppose there was something like that around, I'll check with the boys." The commissioner was not interested in this at all. "We've turned everything over to the FBI, and it's theirs from here on in."

"I don't suppose DiCastro has made any statement?"

"I talked to Colby this morning and he said no. He said that DiCastro opened up a little when he first went in to see him and that he said he had been framed—that sooner or later the truth would come out. Well, that's to be expected. He'd naturally say he was framed."

"Did Colby tell him about finding the bonds in the mattress?"

"Yes. He made his denial right after that."

"Anything else, commissioner?"

Buell shook his head and took a cigar from the box in his desk. "That's all for now. I'll let you know what I hear from Colby."

Pete got up. "Thanks, commissioner. Will you let me know about that needle and thread?"

"Sure."

Pete returned to the *Press* office and told Browne of the latest development.

"Is it safe to save it?" asked the city editor. "That's a hell of a big break against DiCastro, you know. It's the final confirmation of Judy's story, and it gives the motive."

"Nobody else will get it," Pete assured him.

"We'll make it the lead for the Sunday *Press* then. You're going to write the story later, aren't you?"

"This afternoon," said Pete. "I want to find out a few more things first."

Pete went back to his desk and started to read the stories in all of the other papers to see if they had any new angles, or had interpreted the old ones differently from his own. Then his phone rang and it was Fran Addams.

"I want to see you," said Pete. "Are you free?"

"I'm uptown. Why don't you come up and we'll have lunch at some decent place? I'm so sick of that coffee shop slop."

Pete met Fran at a small French restaurant on 56th Street called Chez Marie, and they sat at a banquette in the rear of the long loom and ordered a *paté maison* and *coq au vin* and a bottle of Montrachet that was much too expensive.

Fran said, "What did you want to see me about, Pete?"

Pete evaded her question. He said, "Buell's men found those bonds of Judy's. There were a thousand of them missing. They were sewn into DiCastro's mattress."

"I guess that does it for Vincent, eh?" she said.

"That's the way it looks right now... How was Judy?"

"Last night? The same as usual. She's always the same."

"Why'd you write that kind of a story, Fran?"

She gave a small shrug, a bare movement of her shoulders. "What other kind of story could I write?"

Their *paté* arrived and they began to eat. Pete said, "You don't want to tell the truth about Judy Hinemann, do you?"

"That doesn't belong in a family newspaper," replied Fran with a laugh.

"Maybe not, not the whole truth. But you could have let a little of it slip out, couldn't you?"

"I know," said Fran. "You didn't like my story."

"It was a beautiful story," said Pete. "It made mine read like an account of a town board meeting in Dutchess County. That isn't what I'm talking about, I'm talking about Judy Starr Hinemann."

"She's still a good actress—the best," said Fran. "I don't think there's anyone that girl couldn't deceive—except perhaps myself."

"Nobody would think so."

"She's plausible, Pete, very plausible. She never overplays. She keeps it down on the level of casual communication, without any particular emphasis, and you are very quickly lulled into a mood of acceptance."

"Gordon Buell called her a hard-faced blonde."

"She's that, all right, although few would notice it. She's got all the beauty and the glitter of a diamond and she's just as hard. It shows in her face, but not if you look at her soft, appealing mouth and watch her full lips caress the words as she speaks to you. No, you've got to ignore all of that and look into her green eyes at an unguarded moment. Then you'll see it... But Buell accepted her story, didn't he?"

"Well, what are we going to do about her?"

"We? Nothing. What can *we* do?"

"She's the story, not DiCastro," said Pete.

Fran shuddered. "I was afraid you were going to say that."

"She's like a black widow spider," said Pete. "She devours her males. I don't know too much about her early ones—her first husband, Arthur Winfield, and Dutch Froelich—but Angelo Scotti is dead, and I bet the other two are carrying scars to this day. Her recent record is pretty fair. Lamar Hinemann is dead. Vincent DiCastro is as good as dead. No matter what happens, he'll never get over this. Luke Wardell is a human wreck. I saw him the other night, and I don't think he's going to recover from her. Larry Keene thinks he will, but I think Larry is wrong."

"That's not very much to go on, is it?" said Fran.

"Oh, there's a lot more than that," said Pete. "Everybody's ignored the one most important factor of all, up to now. I got to thinking about it last night while I was trying to go to sleep, and I suddenly realized that I had been just as blind as all the rest.

"It all comes back to the three killings—Gower, Aganna and Joe Bird. There's no doubt that these three were done in by the syndicate, by the crime organization. One of Buell's men, O'Malley, found that out definitely about Gower and Aganna. He even knows who the two men are who were brought up here from New Orleans to do the job.

"They don't know who killed Joe Bird, true enough, but that's got 'syndicate' written all over it. They might as well have autographed it. So, if the syndicate was in it, then that leaves out Vincent DiCastro. He's got no more connections with the syndicate than I have."

"And Judy Hinemann has, I suppose," scoffed Fran.

"Sure," said Pete. "She's been collecting $2,500 a month from the boys ever since the demise of Angelo Scotti, her first New York lover."

"How do you know that?"

"FBI report."

"Well, if they know it, what are they waiting for?"

"That's the jack-pot question," said Pete. "What do you say we try to find out?"

"It's worth it," said Fran. "It'll be a good story."

"That," said Pete, "is the understatement of the century."

After they had ordered their dessert and coffee, Pete went to the telephone booth in the front of the restaurant and called Gordon Buell. He got Buell at his home and told him, "I want to see Calvin Colby as soon as possible. Can you arrange it for me?"

Buell said, "Why don't you arrange it yourself, Pete? Just call him."

"No, you do it," said Pete. "You tell him that we're on to something—that we've got to protect ourselves and that he's got to talk to us."

Buell was silent for a moment. "You catch on pretty fast, don't you?"

"Sometimes," said Pete.

"There wasn't any needle and thread," said Buell.

"That's what I thought."

"All right, I'll phone him. You call me back in a few minutes."

Pete returned to the table. "We're on the right track now, Fran," he said. "Let's go."

Pete paid the waiter and helped Fran on with her coat. Then he retrieved his own from the checkroom and went back into the phone booth. He got Buell immediately.

"You go down there right now," said Buell. "He's at Church Street and he's waiting for you."

"Thanks," said Pete.

They got a cab outside the restaurant and rode downtown, Fran said, "You seem to be so sure of yourself, Pete. Suppose you're wrong?"

"I'm not wrong," said Pete. "When I read all you had written about Judy this morning, I suddenly began to see just what kind of person she was pretending to be. You had all of that perfectly, her fear of DiCastro and her inability to cope with the problem of her husband's death and her loneliness. All of that was the role the new Judy Starr was playing, right up to the hilt. The trouble was that none of it, not one of her attitudes or posings, had anything at all to do with the girl who had slept around with gangsters and had profited with a life annuity of $2,500 a month through the murder of one of them. You couldn't possibly reconcile this Judy of your story with the Judy who had deliberately married such a man as Lamar Hinemann."

"No," agreed Fran, "you couldn't. I thought about that, too. I wondered which Judy Hinemann I should write about—the girl who was before me sobbing out her fears or the girl I knew her to be. Then I decided to take her as she was presenting herself and put her down on paper."

Special Agent in Charge Calvin Colby met them at the door to the FBI office and escorted them through an empty reception room and down a long hall to a small office overlooking a courtyard. He held a chair for Fran Addams and then went behind a metal desk and sat. There were just the three of them.

Pete said, "The *Press* has established certain rights in this airliner sabotage story, Mr. Colby. I concede that they are very tenuous...that perhaps 'rights' is not the proper word. However, we have worked with Mr. Buell and we have brought about, with our stories, the present situation regarding the solution of this sabotage."

Colby nodded his head in agreement. "You have been a great help to us," he said. "I do not deny that."

"Now we are at the end of this affair," Pete said, "and I think it would be unfair if we were forced to share on an equal basis with all the other newspapers a final solution we have helped to bring about."

"I don't know that I follow you, Mr. Morehouse," said the FBI man.

"I'm talking about tomorrow's story—or Monday's," said Pete. "I want it exclusive for the *Press.*"

"And what will this story you believe will occur tomorrow or Monday be, Mr. Morehouse?"

"The arrest of Judy Starr Hinemann for placing the time bomb aboard Flight 900 of Oceanic Airways, Mr. Colby."

Calvin Colby tapped a pencil on his desk and looked at his moving fingers. Then he raised his eyes to Pete's and smiled slightly. "You have kept up with us remarkably well," he said. "You were even ahead of us with Gower and Aganna, although we had those two on our agenda when Mr. Buell first called me... Tell me why you believe the arrest of Mrs. Hinemann is imminent?"

"Because of her background—her connection with organized crime, known as the syndicate," said Pete promptly. "Also because Vincent DiCastro has no such connection."

"How about Luke Wardell?" asked Colby.

Pete shook his head. "No, he won't do. I talked to him. He hasn't got the qualifications to do this sort of thing."

Colby's smile broadened. "We'd get nowhere in this business, Mr. Morehouse, if we operated on your system. You'd need evidence before you could make an arrest, whether it was Luke Wardell or Mrs. Hinemann. Let's talk about evidence, not how you feel about people."

Pete scratched his head, then lit a cigarette. "That is your business, to collect evidence," he said. "Mine is merely that of a newspaper reporter. I'm not a detective. Sure, sometimes I smell out a story. I get a good hunch what it is and where I'll find it, but I can't collect evidence. I don't know how. Miss Addams is the one who gave me the real tip-off on Judy Hinemann. It was her story in Friday's *Press*. Perhaps you read it. This was a story of what Judy Hinemann wanted the world to believe she was. This was the story of a person hiding a great guilt and an overwhelming fear, not the fear of DiCastro but a fear of being found out for what she was and what she had done. Now as for evidence, I have no doubt that there's been plenty of that lying around and that by this time you've got it all. That story of the 40,000 shares of negotiable and unregistered bonds, for instance. Those bonds ought to produce some real good evidence, shouldn't they?"

Colby nodded. "They did," he said. "A surprising aspect of that was that she held out the missing 1,000 bonds for herself—and put them in her own safe deposit box Friday an hour or so before she came downtown to tell her story to Gordon Buell. She was too greedy. It was not intelligent."

"Another thing I was wondering about," said Pete. "Sewing up those bonds in the mattress. That's too obvious. That's detective-story stuff. People with any sense wouldn't do that. I mean, DiCastro certainly wouldn't, as smart as he's supposed to be. So I asked Mr. Buell whether he'd found a sewing kit in DiCastro's apartment. He said he hadn't."

"No," said Colby, "there was none. But we have matched the thread used to sew the mattress with a spool found in Mrs. Hineman's apartment."

"Well, that is evidence—that's the kind of stuff a newspaper reporter can't go out and get. When are you going to pick up Mrs. Hinemann, Mr. Colby?"

"At 10:00 tonight," he said. "You can have your story written, and you can beat all of the other Sunday papers with it for an hour or so. That's the best I can do, Mr. Morehouse."

Pete and Fran got up and shook Colby's hand. He walked to the lobby door with them. On the way down in the elevator Pete said to Fran, "Now you can write the real story of you-know-who."

Fran nodded. She said, "It's going to be a story that will singe your hair."

THE END

If you've enjoyed this book, you will not want to miss these terrific titles…

ARMCHAIR MYSTERY & SCIENCE FICTION CLASSICS
$12.95 each

If you've enjoyed this book, you will not want to miss these terrific titles...

ARMCHAIR SCI-FI & HORROR DOUBLE NOVELS, $12.95 each

D-1   **THE GALAXY RAIDERS** by William P. McGivern
          SPACE STATION #1 by Frank Belknap Long

D-2   **THE PROGRAMMED PEOPLE** by Jack Sharkey
          SLAVES OF THE CRYSTAL BRAIN by William Carter Sawtelle

D-3   **YOU'RE ALL ALONE** by Fritz Leiber
          THE LIQUID MAN by Bernard C. Gilford

D-4   **CITADEL OF THE STAR LORDS** by Edmond Hamilton
          VOYAGE TO ETERNITY by Milton Lesser

D-5   **IRON MEN OF VENUS** by Don Wilcox
          THE MAN WITH ABSOLUTE MOTION by Noel Loomis

D-6   **WHO SOWS THE WIND...** by Rog Phillips
          THE PUZZLE PLANET by Robert A. W. Lowndes

D-7   **PLANET OF DREAD** by Murray Leinster
          TWICE UPON A TIME by Charles L. Fontenay

D-8   **THE TERROR OUT OF SPACE** by Dwight V. Swain
          QUEST OF THE GOLDEN APE by Paul W. Fairman & Milton Lesser

D-9   **SECRET OF MARRACOTT DEEP** by Henry Slesar
          PAWN OF THE BLACK FLEET by Mark Clifton.

D-10 **BEYOND THE RINGS OF SATURN** by Robert Moore Williams
          A MAN OBSESSED by Alan E. Nourse

ARMCHAIR SCIENCE FICTION CLASSICS, $12.95 each

C-1   **THE GREEN MAN**
          by Harold M. Sherman

C-2   **A TRACE OF MEMORY**
          By Keith Laumer

C-3   **INTO PLUTONIAN DEPTHS**
          by Stanton A. Coblentz

ARMCHAIR MASTERS OF SCIENCE FICTION SERIES, $16.95 each

M-1   **MASTERS OF SCIENCE FICTION, Vol. One**
          Bryce Walton—"Dark of the Moon" and other tales

M-2   **MASTERS OF SCIENCE FICTION, Vol. Two**
          Jerome Bixby—"One Way Street" and other tales

If you've enjoyed this book, you will not want to miss these terrific titles…

ARMCHAIR SCI-FI & HORROR DOUBLE NOVELS, $12.95 each

D-91   **THE TIME TRAP** by Henry Kuttner
        THE LUNAR LICHEN by Hal Clement

D-92   **SARGASSO OF LOST STARSHIPS** by Poul Anderson
        THE ICE QUEEN by Don Wilcox

D-93   **THE PRINCE OF SPACE** by Jack Williamson
        POWER by Harl Vincent

D-94   **PLANET OF NO RETURN** by Howard Browne
        THE ANNIHILATOR COMES by Ed Earl Repp

D-95   **THE SINISTER INVASION** by Edmond Hamilton
        OPERATION TERROR by Murray Leinster

D-96   **TRANSIENT** by Ward Moore
        THE WORLD-MOVER by George O. Smith

D-97   **FORTY DAYS HAS SEPTEMBER** by Milton Lesser
        THE DEVIL'S PLANET by David Wright O'Brien

D-98   **THE CYBERENE** by Rog Phillips
        BADGE OF INFAMY by Lester del Rey

D-99   **THE JUSTICE OF MARTIN BRAND** by Raymond A. Palmer
        BRING BACK MY BRAIN by Dwight V. Swain

D-100   **WIDE-OPEN PLANET** by L. Sprague de Camp
        AND THEN THE TOWN TOOK OFF by Richard Wilson

ARMCHAIR SCIENCE FICTION CLASSICS, $12.95 each

C-31   **THE GOLDEN GUARDSMEN**
        by S. J. Byrne

C-32   **ONE AGAINST THE MOON**
        by Donald A. Wollheim

C-33   **HIDDEN CITY**
        by Chester S. Geier

ARMCHAIR SCI-FI & HORROR GEMS SERIES, $12.95 each

G-9   **SCIENCE FICTION GEMS, Vol. Five**
        Clifford D. Simak and others

G-10   **HORROR GEMS, Vol. Five**
        E. Hoffman Price and others